KINTANA
~ and the ~
CAPTAIN'S CURSE

"I really enjoyed my voyage through the pages of Kintana
and the Captain's Curse. Smelly pirates, dastardly plots,
a generous pinch of magic and an entire menagerie of
exotic animals made for the perfect sailing/reading
companions! A fine treasure of a book!"

JENNY MOORE

"Ahoy there, me hearties! Watch out for this swashbuckling
adventure by Susan Brownrigg! It had me talking like
a pirate all day! Curses and charms, cutlasses and
treasure chests! Such fun!"

EVE MCDONNELL

Susan Brownrigg

KINTANA
~ and the ~
CAPTAIN'S
CURSE

Illustrated by
JENNY CZERWONKA

uclanpublishing

Kintana and the Captain's Curse is a uclanpublishing book

First published in Great Britain in 2021 by
uclanpublishing
University of Central Lancashire
Preston, PR1 2HE, UK

978-1-912979-56-1

1 3 5 7 9 10 8 6 4 2

Set in 10/16pt Kingfisher

A CIP catalogue record for this book is available from the British Library.

Printed and bound in Great Britain by Clays Ltd, Elcograf S.p.A.

For Max

NOSY
BORAHA

Ikalalao Forest

Ambodifototra

Pirate Cemetery

Nosy Nato

PIRATE
ISLAND

Trading Post

Leaky Boat Inn

Pirate Island Harbour

Pirate Island Pet Shop

Crossing to Nosy Boraha

THE ANIMALS OF THE ISLANDS

MOUSE LEMUR

INDRI LEMUR

GIANT MADAGASCAR
TORTOISE

FOSSA

ELEPHANT BIRD

GIANT MALAGASY
JUMPING RAT

GREATER VASA PARROT

AYE AYE

Pirate Island
Nosy Boraha
Madagascar
1733

Chapter One

A NEW RECRUIT

K INTANA PANNED PA'S SPYGLASS ACROSS THE TALL
ship's sails. A black flag fluttered on the mast! *Pirates!*
She nearly toppled off her ladder with excitement. She
pictured herself on board the ship fearlessly slashing at enemies
in a ferocious cutlass battle.

Kintana gave the pet shop sign another quick wipe and scooted
to the ground. She tightened her bandana over her black braids,
then ran inside to a cacophony of squawking, hooting and howling
and the familiar smell of grass bedding and animal feed.

"There's a ship entering the harbour," Kintana shouted to Pa.
She had to get a closer look! How could you grow up on Pirate
Island and not crave a life on the sea? She wanted sea monsters
and shipwrecks, typhoons and treasure, not mucking out and
feeding time. "I could sell some animals to the crew."

"I thought you'd agreed to steer clear of pirates, Kintana."

"But we need the money, besides you're a pirate, Pa!"

"An ex-pirate," he corrected.

It was true, Pa was a pet shop owner now, but he still looked like a pirate! He wore a blue bandana over his scruffy blond hair and was dressed in a white shirt, open from his pale pink neck to his navel, and yellow trousers that were cropped short above the knee so you could see one hairy leg and one wooden one.

"We haven't sold an animal in weeks – I have to try," said Kintana. "They might take the fanaloka." She gazed at the sleeping striped civet. "I'll tell them it is an excellent mouser. I could take some of those tenrecs too before they breed any more! I've a feeling our fortune is going to change today."

"Ooh, perhaps that means someone will finally buy that pygmy hippo?" said Pa, leaning against the shop counter.

"You hope so." Kintana picked up a cabbage and tossed it into the hippo's pen. "If he doesn't sell soon, he'll eat us out of house and home *and* shop. I thought we'd agreed to only sell small species!"

"He *is* small, Kintana, for a hippo."

"Very funny, Pa. But seriously, if we don't make more sales soon, we won't be able to afford food for us *or* the animals."

Pa sighed. "All right, but we have to finish tidying first, in case we do get some customers."

Kintana squealed and hugged him tight. Then she raced from one cage to the next, like a whirlwind, emptying water and food bowls in one move, refilling them in the next.

The birds sang, the rodents squeaked, and the lemurs waved their long black-and-white-striped tails at her.

Pa rubbed his sleeve along the counter. Crumbs of nuts, seeds, crackers and biscuits fell to the ground. He scurried around to the other side; his wooden leg rarely slowed him down.

Kintana started to scoop the mess up, "Oh! Pa! I'd already done the floor."

He grinned, revealing a smattering of teeth. "Had you? Sorry, Kintana." He took the handful of rubbish from her and threw it out the window.

Her mouth fell open. "I'll clean that up, too, shall I?"

"I'm in the way, aren't I? Let me fetch you the hand cart," said Pa.

Kintana nodded and set about selecting which other creatures to take to the harbour. The night heron, a panther chameleon, a pair of day geckos, and some more small mammals – a bokiboky, the vontsira and half a dozen big-footed mice. One by one, she lugged their cages into a pile.

"You had better take some animal food, too," said Pa, wheeling in the cart. "I imagine the crew has lots of pets already so, even if they don't want to buy another animal, they might still want food and treats."

Kintana gathered sacks of seed, corn and fresh leaves to take and began to stack them on the cart. "Are you coming with me?"

"And miss out on selling that pygmy hippo? No, I'll stay here. Besides you're twelve years old now – you don't need me holding your hand any longer."

Kintana swallowed. She and Pa did everything together, but recently she'd pushed for more freedom. Now she was being granted it, she suddenly felt a bit nervous.

Kintana had been nine when Mama died after a short illness. Right up until the end, she had insisted on braiding Kintana's hair.

Now Pa looked after it, did the cooking, bought her clothes and listened when she was upset or worried.

Pa's right. I am old enough to look after myself, she realised. *So why do I feel I'm the one that needs convincing?*

☠

Kintana didn't have far to walk before she reached the harbour but dragging a heavy cart full of pets for sale made it hard work. She took off her lamba and draped it over the cages. The animals would prefer the shade under the shawl.

The Nine Sails was enormous! A beautiful brigantine. 90 foot long with two masts, furled sails, and a seahorse figurehead.

Kintana looked up at the crow's nest, there was no tell-tale flag now but *The Nine Sails* was definitely a pirate ship.

The crew on deck wore brightly coloured shirts, breeches and bandanas. Flintlock pistols on silk ribbon dangled around their necks while cutlasses – short swords, ideal for fighting in tight spaces – hung at their waists. Others were stripped to the navel, as they groaned and cursed while cleaning the seaweed and barnacles off the hull.

Suddenly, her view was blocked. A pirate with bronzed skin, eyes like jet and wiry grey hair worn in a plait had stepped in front of her. He wore a blue jacket over a green waistcoat, dark trousers and a red bandana. She winced at the pong of dirt and stale sweat.

"My name's Gangrene, Quartermaster of *The Nine Sails*." He pushed out his chin proudly. "We need supplies, especially fresh food. What've you got hidden on that cart, boy?"

"I'm not a . . ." Kintana hesitated to correct him. She needed a sale.

"Somethin' bothering you?" Gangrene asked, breathing a repulsive stench over her.

She grimaced. "No, sir."

"Huh." The pirate lifted the lamba and peered inside the cages. "I'm selling pets."

"I can see that." He grunted. "We've got all the pets we need, too many in fact."

"Don't you like animals?"

"Did I say that?" he scowled, "No, I just mean they need a lot of lookin' after – they're not all as well behaved as my Snuffles." The man opened his waistcoat to reveal a small rodent. It had short grey fur, long pink ears and a pink, ribbed tail like a worm.

"A baby votsotsa!" she exclaimed.

"He's not a votswhatsnot, he's a Giant Jumpin' Rat," said Gangrene, rolling his eyes.

"Oh, we have a different name for them here," Kintana smiled. "He's adorable."

Gangrene's face softened. "Isn't he? I found him abandoned, poor mite." The pirate kissed his pet on the top of its head, "You love your daddy, don't you, Snuffles?"

Poor Snuffles, the sight of that kiss made Kintana feel quite queasy.

"What about a lovely chameleon?" she asked, hopefully. "You won't even notice it on board!" she joked. "Get it? Chameleons blend in with their surroundings . . ."

"I *told* you, we don't need more blinkin' animals. We're only here to quickly restock, repair and recruit. Captain Tortuga has heard a big merchant ship is heading this way and he means to attack within days. I need crew not creatures."

Kintana grabbed his arm. "I'm a pirate! Hire me!"

"*You?*" Gangrene scoffed. He stroked Snuffles's head.

"I am!"

"Hmm . . . I bet you'd faint at the sight of a nosebleed. You're too scrawny and weak to be of much use. What's your name?"

"Kintana."

"What kind of a name is that?"

"It's Malagasy. It means star." Her cheeks flushed.

"Well, Kintana," he leaned forward and scanned her from head to toe. "You fancy yourself as a cabin boy, do you?"

Kintana couldn't look at his face. The quartermaster wouldn't give her a job if he knew she was a girl. Some pirates thought women were bad luck on ships, even though there had been female buccaneers like Mary Read and Anne Bonny.

"I'm good at lots of things," Kintana insisted. "I am very organised; I prepare the animals' food and water, I clean their cages and treat them if they get sick."

"Really? Perhaps there is a job suitable for you." Gangrene spat on the floor; a big, green lump of phlegm just missing Kintana's shoes. "Well pirates aren't very different to animals. As cabin boy you would assist the cook, run errands for the captain. Scrub decks, mend sails . . . and I suppose you could assist with the captain's collection."

Kintana's eyes widened as big as a mouse lemur's. "Yes, sir!"

Gangrene wiped his nose on his sleeve. "You're hired. Get your belongings . . . be here at dawn, we set sail tomorrow."

Chapter Two

BREAKING THE NEWS

THE ANIMALS SQUAWKED, GRUNTED AND SQUEAKED as Kintana pulled the cart home. Her village seemed different as she approached. Smaller. Shabbier.

A log stockade surrounded the few buildings. She walked past the Leaky Boat tavern and the general trading post to the pet shop.

It was midday, and Pa had closed the shutters on the shop. The smell of roasting vegetables welcomed Kintana at the front door. She wheeled the cart inside, trying not to sneeze as a duck feather wafted around her nose.

Kintana began putting the animal cages back in position. She had a feeling Pa wouldn't be too disappointed that she hadn't sold any animals. He hadn't wanted her to go to the harbour in the first place. He'd enjoy saying, 'I told you so.'

"I'm putting lunch on the table . . ." he called.

"I'm coming." Kintana ran into the room and swung herself onto a chair opposite Pa, licking her lips at the smell of coconut and ginger. She shovelled delicious yam into her mouth.

"Did you sell any animals?"

She shook her head.

"Never mind," he smiled. "I didn't sell the hippo, either."

They continued to eat in silence. Kintana kept rehearsing in her head how to tell Pa about *The Nine Sails*, Gangrene *and* the job. None of her attempts felt right.

"Something botherin' you, love?"

Kintana looked down at her pewter plate – this was her cue. She fished out a piece of ginger from her tooth with her tongue. "I've got a job," she said quietly.

"A job?" Pa repeated. "What do you mean? Have you banged your head on a cage? You already have a job. You work with me in the pet shop."

"I mean a *new* job," Kintana mumbled.

Pa sniffed loudly and started gathering up the plates, busying himself. "Not the Trading Post; you wouldn't swap one shop for another."

"No, Pa. Of course not."

"Please tell me you're not going to be serving drinks in the Leaky Boat! I won't have a daughter of mine working in that tavern!"

"You like it enough in there. Anyway, my job's not on Pirate Island."

"Not on Pirate Island? What do you mean? Surely you're not going to be crossing to Nosy Boraha every day?" Pa gasped overdramatically. "I know . . . you're goin' to be a gravedigger at the pirate cemetery!" he teased.

"Don't be silly, Pa."

He winked. "There's always work for gravediggers, Kintana."

She laughed despite herself. Then she took a deep breath. "I'm going further away . . ."

"Not Madagascar itself!" he clasped a hand to his face.

"Further . . ." she lowered her voice, "I'm going to be a pirate."

Pa dropped the plates, the metal clattering. He staggered to a chair, slumping on to it. "A pirate, Kintana? What? When? How?" His mouth kept opening and closing but no more sounds came out.

"It's what I've always wanted." Kintana got up and went over to him, hugging him tight. "Please Pa. I want to be a pirate, like you used to be."

"No, Kintana! You don't. That way of life always costs you somethin'. It cost me my leg, nearly my life. I almost ended up a beggar. If I hadn't been pardoned and given the chance to come to this island. If I hadn't met your beautiful, kind, lovely mama . . ."

"I thank God I'm not a pirate any longer. I run a pet shop. If you want to be like me, you'll stay here and carry on looking after the animals." Pa stood and picked up the plates again. "Help me tidy up this mess," he sighed.

Kintana scraped the leftovers into a bucket.

When they had finished, Pa told Kintana to sit down. "It's time you knew the truth."

Her stomach felt heavy, and not from food. She pulled up a chair next to Pa.

He patted his wooden leg. "I haven't stepped aboard a ship since 1718."

Kintana was puzzled, she already knew the story well. "The Battle of Ocracoke."

"Captain Blackbeard was unbeatable, everyone knew that. Even with twenty cutlass wounds and five pistol shots to his body, he was still convinced he would win—"

Kintana picked up the tale. "Blackbeard was mortally wounded, but you survived, Pa, *even though* he'd shot you in the knee to keep you and the other pirates in line! You were stronger than him, braver than him, a better pirate!"

He covered his face. "No. The truth is, I was a coward, Kintana. I should have protected him, but instead I hid – and then I watched Blackbeard slide to the floor, moanin', his life drainin' away. I crawled over to him. I was in such pain . . ."

Kintana took Pa's hand. "Go on . . ."

He closed his eyes, remembering. "I tore off my shirt, tried to stem the bleeding, but there was so much blood. Blackbeard pushed me away at first – *A few stitches from the Doc', a swig of grog and I'll be back at the helm, Israel.* Then he pulled me close, wrenched off his hat and looked deep into my eyes . . . He tried to speak again, but it was too late. Blackbeard died just like every other pirate, messily. I will not allow that to happen to you. I'm sorry, Kintana, but you won't be goin'. You have to stay on Pirate Island."

☠

Kintana stormed out of the room and flung herself on to her bed. Tears of anger burned her cheeks.

It was so unfair that she had to stay on the island. There had to be a way to make Pa change his mind.

She could hear him pacing up and down.

What reason could she give for going?

Then his footsteps stopped.

Pa rapped quietly on her door.

He leaned into her room, then came to perch next to her on the bed. "Aren't you happy here, Kintana?"

She sniffed, trying not to cry.

"I know you miss Mama, but I try to be a good father," he continued, as he reached for her hand, his clasp firm, his skin rough with calluses from years of reefing sails. "You look so much like her."

Kintana clamped her lips together. He looked so sad. *No*, she thought, she had to try and remain angry with him. She turned her face away.

"Ah, Kintana, why do things have to change? I wish your Mama was still here. I wish you weren't growin' up so quickly."

Kintana let out a sob. "But I *am* growing up, Pa."

He nodded. "And . . ."

"*And* I want to see the world. I want to see more than just this island."

Pa put his hand on her shoulder. "Ah, but there are things out there I don't want you to see. The world isn't like home, Kintana. It's big and cruel and dangerous and hard—"

"And thrilling and exciting and, and, oh, *please*, Pa?"

He stared at her. She could see Pa was torn.

Kintana tried one more plea. "I have to find out for myself, Pa. You can't protect me from life."

Pa blinked hard, took out a hanky and blew his nose. "If you really want to go, I'll let you. I would rather give you my blessin' than have you run away to sea."

Kintana threw her arms around him. "Misaotra! Thank you!"

"I suppose I should help you pack; at least I know what a pirate requires. Cutlass. Handkerchief. Rum. On second thoughts, maybe not rum." Pa moved across the room and unlocked a tall cabinet. He pulled out a black felt hat and carried it across to Kintana before placing it on her head. "If you're goin' to be a pirate, you'll need a hat."

"Is it yours?" Kintana asked, swelling up with pride, as she put the three-cornered-hat on.

"Well, not exactly, I mean . . . yes, I suppose it is, except it's yours now."

"It's brilliant, Pa." Kintana pulled a long, black hair off it. "How do I look?"

"Beautiful . . . and I'm sure you'll grow into it."

Kintana laughed. "*Paaa!*"

Chapter Three

A MOTLEY CREW

PEERING OUT FROM UNDER HER NEW HAT, KINTANA paused at the harbour, as the day dawned. Pa had apologised for not seeing her off – he couldn't face saying goodbye. She was more than a little relieved as she had a feeling he'd have blubbed like a baby.

She adjusted her red jacket and picked up her knapsack, then crossed the gangway on to *The Nine Sails*. There were parrot owners with noses as big as beaks and monkey keepers with long arms and legs, all preparing the ship for sail. Kintana had often thought that people looked like their pets and it was certainly true of *The Nine Sails* pirates.

A bell rang out and the crew suddenly scrambled down the rigging using 'ratlines', rope ladders, while others appeared from hatches.

Gangrene was last to join the rest of the crew, standing next to a Malagasy man in a striped lamba with spiky hair and a tenrec peeping out of his pocket.

"Welcome aboard," Gangrene whispered as Kintana slid in next to him.

She stood up straight and held her breath as a man in a smart white jacket and a leather three-cornered-hat approached.

She noticed he was the only man without a pet.

"Good mornin', Captain Tortuga!" said Gangrene.

"Good morning, Mr Gangrene." The captain took off his hat for a moment and rubbed his bald head. "Is this the new recruit you told me about?"

"Yes, Captain."

The captain's watery blue eyes locked on to Kintana. "You are very fortunate to be taken under Mr Gangrene's wing."

"Yes, Captain."

Tortuga smiled and turned away from Kintana, his eyes falling on the spiky-haired tenrec owner. "Let's hope the crew has good health on our voyage, Dokotera."

"Eny, yes, Captain," he replied, running a hand over his spiky hair.

"Spike is a great sawbones," whispered Gangrene. "He's good with poultices and potions too. You should see his medicine chest! It's full of herbs and spices. He can fix everythin' from a runny nose to a broken leg."

Kintana swallowed and hoped she wouldn't need his services.

Tortuga was now facing a sunburnt red-haired pirate with a tomato frog popping out of his pocket. "Croak. I am glad you have agreed to be our new navigator."

The man's cheeks reddened more. "Mr Gangrene was very persuasive," he replied, with a raspy voice.

"Yes, well it is a position notoriously difficult to fill."

"What happened to the old navigator?" whispered Kintana.

"It's a sad tale." Gangrene crossed himself. "Last time we were on Pirate Island, Eyeball went treasure huntin' over on Nosy Boraha. He was missin' for days. When he did finally return, the poor soul was scratched all over, dehydrated and delirious. I put him in my cabin to rest. While I was fetchin' the dokotera I heard a terrible splash – the fool had leapt overboard."

"How awful." Kintana shook her head.

"Heart-breakin'," replied Gangrene.

Tortuga moved on to a pale, skinny boy with a giant turquoise stick insect on his jacket lapel. Beads of sweat ran down his pimpled face. "Ah, Bartholomew . . ."

The boy stammered, "Y-yes, Captain Tortuga."

"Remind me, Bartholomew, what is the most important part of being a lookout?"

"Being awake?"

"Well, yes, we *have* had that discussion. Try again . . ."

"Oh! A lookout must always be in position."

"And *where* is that?"

"In the crow's nest, Captain."

"So, why are you not up there . . ." Tortuga jabbed a thumb at the top of the mainmast, "looking out there?" He gestured to the vast Indian Ocean.

"I was looking for Blackbeard, sir."

Kintana closed her eyes in embarrassment for the boy. He clearly wasn't very bright.

"Blackbeard?" repeated the captain. "What are you on about?"

"I heard his footsteps on deck," the boy continued.

"Dead men don't make footsteps," said Croak, sniggering.

The other pirates burst into laughter.

"His spirit does! I've heard him. He stalks the deck at night."

Gangrene stamped his feet slowly, mimicking ghostly footsteps.

"It's not funny," Bartholomew wailed. "Everyone knows Blackbeard was cursed to spend the afterlife looking for his—"

Gangrene stamped his feet again, stretched his arms out, and gave an eerie moan. "Ooohhhh."

"Stop it! I'm telling the truth. Ask Pots, if you don't believe me. He's smelled smoke on deck – only there's never any fire."

"More likely he burned something again down in the galley," quipped Spike.

"It is Blackbeard," insisted Bartholomew. "Everyone knows the captain used to light tapers in his hair and beard when attacking a ship – he must have looked terrifying surrounded by smoke!"

"*Enough!*" the captain interrupted.

"Why would Blackbeard's ghost be haunting a ship in the middle of the Indian Ocean?" asked Kintana. "He died in North Carolina – that's thousands of miles away."

"Because they threw his body overboard," continued Bartholomew, "and now he's cursed to spend eternity searching—"

"What, and he swam all the way to Madagascar?" Tortuga grunted.

"It's just one of the crew playin' a silly prank," said Gangrene.

"Hmm," the captain licked his dry lips. "Bartholomew, this is your final warning. You are demoted – from now on, you're on laundry duties."

Bartholomew grumbled to himself. "But it wasn't my fault, Captain—" The quartermaster put his hand over the boy's mouth.

"Listen here!" the captain bellowed. "One more mention of Blackbeard, a Captain's Curse or ghosts and you will be flogged."

Kintana winced at the thought of the boy being whipped.

The boy squeaked: "Yes, Captain, I mean no, Captain."

Tortuga pulled his hat down tighter onto his head. "Now, back to your duties, men."

The pirates scurried away like beetles seeking an old log to hide under.

Gangrene and Kintana remained, Bartholomew hovering at their side.

"Mr Gangrene, I will see you and the new cabin boy in my study," said the captain. "But first, please ask Pots to prepare a bowl of stew for my evening meal."

"Yes, Captain."

"Laundry duties!" Gangrene grabbed Bartholomew by the lughole as soon as Tortuga was out of sight. "You're no good to me scourin' dirty slops day and night."

Kintana winced.

"Sorry, Mr Gangrene." Bartholomew's eyes filled with tears.

Gangrene let go of the boy's ear and tutted. "At least tell me you've completed my three challenges?"

"Not y-yet, Mr Gangrene, sir," he stammered. "I'm not good with riddles." He stared at the floor. "It would be easier if you just gave me a list of the things you need me to find."

"Then, it would hardly be a challenge, would it?"

"No, Mr Gangrene, sir," replied Bartholomew.

Kintana raised an eyebrow. *Why was Bartholomew trying to solve riddles?*

"You are pathetic," snarled Gangrene.

"Please. I can be useful. Let me tell Pots to make the captain's stew, then you can go straight to the captain."

Gangrene rubbed his chin. "Hmm. Now there's an idea . . . Tell Pots to use those special herbs I procured for him. You *can* pass on a simple message, can't you, Bartholomew?"

"Yes, Mr Gangrene, sir." The boy was trembling like a spider web in a gale.

"Off you go then."

Bartholomew nearly tripped over his feet in his haste. Kintana rolled her eyes.

"You could learn a lot from Bartholomew," said Gangrene with a grin, "on what *not* to do."

"He actually believes in the Captain's Curse, doesn't he," said Kintana. "But there isn't really a ghost, is there?"

Chapter Four

THE CAPTAIN'S COLLECTION

"**N**AH!" REPLIED GANGRENE. "THE FELLAS ARE JUST havin' a joke – only Bartholomew's takin' it all too seriously. The crew wanted to scare him a bit, I don't know why, he's a milk puddin' as it is. It was hard enough recruitin' a new navigator, now I need to find a new lookout."

"Is it a difficult job?" asked Kintana.

She didn't see how it could be if it was a position that had been entrusted to Bartholomew.

"Not difficult, but important. A lookout needs to be observant at all times, and not afraid of heights, of course."

"I'm not afraid of heights . . ."

"I like your enthusiasm, Kintana, but it's a big responsibility, and you will have lots of tasks to do for me and the captain."

"I could be a temporary lookout, until you find a fulltime replacement."

Something scuttled across the deck towards Gangrene. It was his Malagasy giant jumping rat.

"Hmm, perhaps." Gangrene scooped Snuffles up, his pet's whiskers tickling his face.

Kintana reached out to pet him.

Gangrene pulled away. "Snuffles only likes me. He's fussy about who holds him."

"Understood."

Snuffles dropped a small coin into his master's hand. Gangrene patted the jumping rat's head. "You wouldn't believe the things Snuffles has found for me; things that were hidden away from the naked eye. Yet there are some things even *he* can't track down.

"Now, it is time you signed your articles . . ."

☠

Captain Tortuga was sitting at a large wooden desk. The sun shone through the study's leaded glass window behind him – casting diamond reflections onto the red flock wallpaper.

Kintana looked round at the floor-to-ceiling shelves crammed full of books. The room smelled of pipe tobacco and leather.

"I have volumes on fables and legends, anatomy, botany, bestiaries as well as bibles and ship's logs," said the captain, proudly.

There were even more books piled on the desk; Gangrene picked up one with the words *Curses and Charms* embossed on the cover, but he put it down sharpish after the captain gave him a look.

Kintana noticed a large globe in the corner of the room and a huge potted palm in another.

"Now, are you ready to sign your articles?" Captain Tortuga

gestured for Kintana to sit in the chair opposite him. A document was waiting for her on the desk, along with an ink pot and quill pen.

"I'm not sure what you know about the process," he continued, "but articles are a document to say you'll follow my rules on behaviour. The usual pirate terms are specified in the contract – fair share of provisions, no drinking and gambling on a Sunday, equal shares from any booty, half shares for boys. If you can't write your name just do a big X."

"My mama was Betsimisaraka. I can read and write in English and Malagasy," said Kintana, dipping the pen nib into the ink before squiggling her signature.

Gangrene slapped her on the shoulder. "Well done, lad."

Kintana felt a rush of excitement. She was officially a pirate!

"Now, would you like to see my collection?" asked Captain Tortuga, standing.

"Yes, Captain," she replied, wondering what he meant.

Tortuga walked over to a heavy green velvet drape that hung at the back of the study. He pulled it to one side.

Kintana peered into the space. Her eyes slowly adjusting to the low light. She gasped. *I thought the captain didn't own a pet – how wrong I was!* The room was filled with animals.

"Welcome to my menagerie! Come . . ."

She followed.

There were glass tanks containing insects, frogs, geckos, chameleons, spiders and snakes. A large aviary held dozens of colourful birds, including flycatchers and vangas - they sang as Kintana leaned closer.

"I am particularly interested in sea life. This is my aquarium . . ." Tortuga added.

There were more glass tanks filled with all different types of shells – some were flat and creamy; others were scalloped and brown. Kintana's favourites were the spirally ones with spots. They moved on to the sea urchins, they looked dangerous with their long sharp spines in black or purple. The next tank contained little fish that darted from side to side in a shoal. In another a large crayfish with grasping claws lay still. A few seemed to contain only barnacles or seaweed.

"This collection is my life's work," said the captain. "It is unrivalled in the world . . ."

At the back of the room were more shelves – but these weren't heavy with books, instead they were filled with stuffed animals, skins, and glass specimen jars. Everything was precisely labelled.

"Most of these items are unique and priceless," said Tortuga.

Kintana inspected a glass dome containing a long brown feather and a glass jar filled with fragments of creamy egg shell marked *Elephant Bird?*

Tortuga leaned in next to her. "Long ago, there were giant lemurs and giant flightless birds living on Madagascar. I often wonder what made them grow so big. The animal world fascinates me. Why does one animal have a long neck," he continued. "Why does the walrus have two tusks," he pointed to a huge spear like tusk, mounted on the wall, "and a narwhal only one? Why can some animals see in the dark? If you eat lion meat, will you become fierce? So many questions . . . but now you must prepare food for my animals – and I must meet with my navigator."

Gangrene bowed. "I'll take the boy to the galley straight away, Captain."

Kintana smiled. She was looking forward to starting work.

Chapter Five

DOWN IN THE GALLEY

A RICH, TANTALISING AROMA OF MEAT EMANATED out from the ship's kitchen. Kintana's mouth watered in anticipation as she followed Gangrene down a couple of steps into a small room filled with wooden shelves containing an array of utensils and supplies.

In the centre of the room was the cook's stove in a brick surround, with a metal chimney to take away the heat and smoke. Bunches of dried herbs dangled from the ceiling.

Bartholomew was sitting at a small wooden table; he had a newly wrapped bandage around three fingers and a thumb.

The cook – a large man – had his back to Kintana, as he put a wooden container high up on a shelf. He turned and smoothed the white moustache that sprouted out from under his nose with his sausage-like fingers. He wore an eyepatch over his left eye.

"That stew smells good," said Gangrene. "Did Bartholomew tell you to use those new herbs?"

"He did. I got him to chop them himself." Pots shook his head despairingly. "Nearly took half his hand off in the process. And his stick insect nearly fell in the stew!"

Kintana grimaced.

"Anyway, I have good news – I have recruited a cabin boy," said Gangrene. "This is Kintana. He cooks, he cleans, and he knows all about animals."

Pots threw a misshapen carrot at Bartholomew and guffawed as it bounced off his head. "You're relieved, in more ways than one."

The boy wailed.

Pots held out a ham-sized arm and clamped Kintana's hand. Her eyes watered as he shook it vigorously. "There's not much muscle on him."

"You'll soon change that," said Gangrene. "Pots has worked with all the best pirate captains; Kidd, Teach – and now Tortuga. You should be honoured to be in his service, Kintana."

"Yes, sir."

"Pots prepares all the food . . . not just for the men, but for their animals too," Gangrene explained. "We don't just have pets, there's farm animals too."

"You do know how to milk a goat, I presume, only Pimples, here, got kicked on the kisser when he tried," said Pots.

Kintana nodded, feeling even sorrier for the boy.

"Good, perhaps I can risk you collecting the eggs too," Pots raised an eyebrow at Bartholomew. "Because we only scramble them when we get them back to the galley."

"Don't worry," replied Gangrene, "Spotty will soon be out from under both our feet. He's already in line for a floggin' with all this talk of curses and ghosts. One more mistake and the captain will have him marooned!"

Oh no! thought Kintana.

She was distracted by something moving under the table. For a moment she thought it was Snuffles again, but this animal was much, much bigger.

"A fossa!" she gasped.

"Her name's Whiskers," said Pots. "Don't worry, she won't bother you as long as you don't get too close. She only bites people who upset her."

The fossa had a muzzle, like a dog, and long, straight whiskers. Her fur was smooth and the colour of soft brown sugar. She was solidly built with a curved back and short legs, especially the front ones, and an extraordinarily long tail.

"She's beautiful," said Kintana. "I thought they were too wild to be kept as pets though."

"Whiskers just needs a little more training to adjust to sea life, but she's proving an excellent ratter. I first spotted her stalking pigs and poultry on the island. She hunts day and night and likes to keep pesky prying pirates away. I keep warning Mr Gangrene to make sure Snuffles doesn't come sniffing around down here."

"She's dangerous," said Gangrene. "A creature like that can't be tamed." He looked uneasily at the fossa. "I thought I told you to keep her in a crate!"

"She needs exercise."

The kitchen was too cramped for such a big animal, the idea of her being kept in a crate was even worse to Kintana.

"At least we were able to get a few more supplies from the tradin' post." said Gangrene, taking a ceramic jar from a shelf and taking off the lid. "I'm sick of weevil-packed hardtack for weeks on end." He pulled out a ship's biscuit and popped it into his mouth.

Whiskers made a strange guttural sound then jumped on to the cook's table and paced back and forth, watching the ground for any signs of movement.

"What's wrong with her?" asked Kintana.

"Maybe she can smell a rat," said Pots, taking the jar from Gangrene before nudging him back towards the stove. "You haven't got Snuffles stuffed inside your shirt again, I hope?"

"Course not." Gangrene pulled his green waistcoat tighter and Kintana could see the shape of the rodent moving under it. "Now, Kintana needs to feed the animals."

"I can help," said Bartholomew. He started filling bowls with seeds and fruit.

The cook pulled a face. "I've told you before, Spotty, you're a hindrance, not a help."

"My name isn't Spotty . . ."

"What was that? Speak up."

"I said my name isn't Spotty, or Pimples," he squeaked, "It's Bartholomew."

"You shouldn't call him names," Kintana muttered.

"Oh, I'm sorry, did I hurt your feelings, *Captain Blackheads*?" said Pots.

"Now, Pots, you heard the boy. Please promise to only use his proper name . . ." said Gangrene, grinning. "Fartolomew! Or Fart for short."

The boy groaned and slumped over the table.

"Right," said Pots. "Kintana – you've got work to do." He passed her a list detailing what each animal on board ate. She needed seeds, nuts, fruit, vegetables and insects. "You'll find water in those barrels."

Kintana sorted out the different dishes and balanced the first lot on a wooden tray.

"Bartholomew, shake yourself, and give the new lad a hand," said Gangrene.

☠

The boy trudged after Kintana on to the deck, mumbling to himself. She couldn't help feeling sorry for him. She tried to spark a conversation. "I like your giant stick insect."

Bartholomew sniffed.

"He's a male, isn't he? The females are rather drab in comparison."

"I call him Sticky. He can change colour," replied the boy quietly. "I wish I could camouflage like him. I'd disappear right into the walls of the ship so no one could ever find me."

"Pots and Gangrene weren't very nice to you," said Kintana, pushing back her hat out of her eyes.

Bartholomew sniffed again. "They're cross with me because I keep making mistakes . . . I'm a rubbish pirate."

She handed a bowl of crickets to a pirate with a beautiful blue coua on his shoulder.

"I'm sure that's not true," she continued, getting a bowl of vegetables ready for a pirate with a pet radiated tortoise.

"It is," insisted Bartholomew. "I can't even solve three simple riddles."

"Oh, yes, Gangrene's challenge. Maybe I can help you work out the answers."

Bartholomew's eyes widened. "Really?"

Kintana shrugged. "I can try."

"I have to find three items. Gangrene has written a riddle for each object. I have to solve each one, locate the items and give them to him. Oh, and no one must see me looking for them."

"Right. So, what is the first riddle?"

"I am a cat with more than one tail," said Bartholomew.

"*A cat with more than one tail?* . . . I know what that is – a cat o'nine tails!"

"Oh! Silly me," said Bartholomew. "I've been looking for a real cat."

Kintana tried not to giggle. The riddle itself had been easy, the tricky part would be finding the whip. "I bet there's one in the captain's study."

"Oh," Bartholomew's shoulders drooped. "Do you think you could find it for me, after all you have to go in there to feed his collection."

She hesitated. "I suppose so . . . what's the next riddle?"

"I am a finger that points to danger."

"Hmm, that's harder. I'll have to think about it."

"It's impossible."

"Give me a chance!" He was very defeatist. "What's the last riddle?"

Bartholomew scratched his head. "Oh yes. I am a skeleton in a nest."

Kintana grinned. "Whatever the object is, it must be in the crow's nest."

"Oh, it would be," he whined. "I'm not allowed up there any more."

"Didn't you notice anything unusual up there, while you were lookout?"

He shook his head. "I give up. I'll tell Gangrene I've failed."

"Wait, there might be another way. *I* could look in the nest. I'll look for the finger too. If I can find all three objects, I'll give them to you – and you can tell Gangrene you solved the riddles yourself."

Bartholomew flung his arms around Kintana. "You're a genius!"

"Easy," she said, pulling back. "You don't want to squash Sticky!"

Chapter Six

THE THREE RIDDLES

KINTANA LEFT BARTHOLOMEW ON DECK AND returned to the Captain's cabin to see to the rest of the pirate pets and Captain Tortuga's collection.

She dished out all the food, according to the list, but now had one bowl of crackers leftover. She double-checked the cook's instructions. Which animal had she missed?

She looked round the menagerie again.

"Under here," squawked a voice.

It was coming from the corner of the room.

Kintana carried the bowl over to a stand with a dome-like top hidden beneath a thick cloth. She yanked it away to reveal a brass birdcage.

Inside was a grey vasa parrot. It studied her with almost human eyes as it chewed on the bar and flashed a grey tongue.

"*Mbola tsara*, hello, I'm Kintana."

It swung down, landing on the bottom of the cage and preened its wings. "*Mbola tsara*. I'm Polly."

She blinked. "I didn't think vasa parrots could talk!"

"Depends who's talking to them," said Polly.

"Who's a pretty Polly," said Kintana.

"Pretty? Handsome you mean," he corrected.

"Isn't Polly a girl's name?"

"Isn't Kintana?" replied the parrot sharply, turning his back.

"Oh, I'm sorry. I didn't mean to offend you."

The parrot tapped its pale beak on the cage catch. "Let me out and I'll forgive you."

Kintana undid the catch and the parrot hopped out and on to her shoulder. His dark talons had a very strong grip.

She looked round for somewhere to put Polly's crackers.

"I usually eat in the captain's study," said the parrot.

"Oh, all right."

☠

Kintana put the bowl of crackers down on top of a big, tea-coloured map which was spread over Captain Tortuga's desk.

Polly hopped on to the map, crunching cracker crumbs as he studied it. "Ah, beautiful Nosy Boraha."

Kintana looked at the long, thin island depicted. There was a bite-like curve at the bottom left and below it an inlet of water with a small round piece of land in the middle – Pirate Island.

Polly closed his eyes. "I can still remember the feeling of freedom on Nosy Boraha as I soared over the palm trees, the aroma of coconut all around. But I belong to the captain now – who knows when I'll ever see my island home again."

"It must be exciting, though," said Kintana. "Travelling to new lands, meeting new people. Having adventures!"

"If you say so. Not that I see much from inside my cage – I miss the breeze in my feathers ..."

"Well, perhaps you could have a little fly around the ship?" suggested Kintana.

"I would love to," said Polly, sadly, "but Gangrene wouldn't like it."

"Why ever not?"

Polly hid his face with a wing. "Because the last time I was allowed out, I accidentally messed on him. He was furious. I tried to tell him, when you've got to go, you've got to go. I didn't realise he was stood in the firing line, honest."

"Oh no!" Kintana chuckled. "Tell you what, if I make sure Gangrene's not around, will you help me with something?"

"Certainly!" Polly picked up another cracker with his talons. "What is it?"

"I have three riddles to solve."

"Is it an initiation challenge?" asked Polly, shaking his head. "Such nonsense."

"I guess so – the answer to each one is an object I have to find. The first riddle is a cat with more than one tail ..."

"Pots has a cat, but I like to stay well away from it!"

"Whiskers is a fossa, not a cat," replied Kintana. "I think the solution is a cat o'nine tails – it's a whip with lots of knotted ropes. I think Captain Tortuga might have one to use for punishments."

She scanned the rest of the desk. There was a magnifying glass, a compass, a spyglass and a brass sextant – but no cat o'nine tails.

Polly lifted a foot and scratched the side of his head. "He might keep one inside his desk drawer."

Kintana took a deep breath. "Do you think I should look?"

Polly flapped his wings. "That's up to you, but if you do, I would be quick about it."

She pulled open the drawer. There was the *Curses and Charms* book, spare quill pens and a pouch of tobacco. She lifted the book and peered underneath.

"Urgh!" Kintana snapped back her hand. Her eyes wide with panic.

"What is it?" asked Polly. "Are you all right?"

Kintana turned away from the desk. "It's . . . it's . . ." she shuddered. "A hand . . . an aye-aye hand."

"Oh, is that all," said Polly.

"You don't understand," said Kintana, trying to blank out the image of the bony lemur hand with its strange long middle finger. "My mama was always afraid of them. She said they are bad luck."

"You don't believe that, do you?"

Her heart was still racing. "I . . . I don't know. It's hard not to believe superstitions."

Kintana swivelled round slowly and lifted the book again. She stared down at the aye-aye hand. It must be part of Captain Tortuga's collection. "It's just a lemur hand," she told herself. "It can't hurt me – Oh! The second riddle, – *a finger that points to danger.*" She groaned. "The answer is the aye-aye finger."

"What are you supposed to do with it?" asked Polly.

"I have to give it to a friend."

"Some present!"

Kintana surveyed the study. "I need something to wrap it in . . . A bandana would work, or a handkerchief . . ."

"You won't find those in here. Try the captain's cabin." He cocked his head towards a doorway that led to Tortuga's berth.

Kintana swallowed nervously. He could be back at any moment. She had to hurry.

☠

The captain had a proper bed, not a hammock, the only other furniture was a wooden chest.

"Search in here," Polly squawked, perching on top. "It will either be clothes or treasure, either way we win!"

Kintana flapped her hands at the parrot to move him, then tugged open the lid hoping there were no more nasty surprises inside.

Hose, shirts, waistcoats, and – oh cravats – perfect. She took a blue one. Then rummaged a little deeper.

Kintana peeled back a sleeve and revealed a cat o'nine tails. She winced, imagining the painful weals the nine knotted ropes would leave when struck across a man's back.

She clasped the leather handle and lifted it to show Polly.

"Make sure you hide it. Captain Tortuga will whip you if he finds you with it."

"He wouldn't!"

"He would."

Kintana bit her lip and shoved the cat o'nine tails inside her jacket.

Then she dashed back into the study and summoned up the courage to take the aye-aye hand. She used the cravat as a kind of barrier and eased it out of the drawer, trying not to squirm as she stuffed it inside her jacket too.

"What's the final riddle?" asked Polly, landing on Kintana's shoulder.

"A skeleton in a nest. Time to head outside."

Chapter Seven

A DIFFERENT PERSPECTIVE

KINTANA WAS SURPRISED TO FIND THE SHIP deserted. "Where is everyone?" she asked.

"The crew must be below decks," said Polly. "They've got to sort all the weaponry and check the ballast is correct before we set sail."

Kintana knew she didn't have much time for the last challenge. She craned her neck to look up at the crow's nest. She felt a bit queasy. She'd never climbed so high.

"Polly," she began, peeling off her shoes. "Will you fly up beside me?" It wasn't too windy on deck, but she knew that it would be a different matter the higher she went.

"Are you sure you want to climb aloft?" asked Polly.

"Yes," said Kintana, even though her head and stomach

disagreed. She checked her hat was on tight.

"Right," said Polly. "The rigging has two parts – the shrouds are vertical, and they hold the masts up. They are nice and strong."

Kintana nodded and grabbed the shrouds above her.

"The ratlines are horizontal. They are for your feet."

Kintana lifted her foot putting it on the first ratline as though it was the rung on a ladder. *One step at a time, that's how I'll do it*, she thought, *and without looking down*.

But unlike a normal ladder, each rope rung bent a little as Kintana stood on it making her feel very unstable. The ratlines swung slightly as she shifted her weight from each foot. She clutched on to the shrouds, the rope rough against her hands, then pulled herself up so she could step on to the next rung. She was sure Gangrene would have been less than impressed by her slow efforts.

Polly encouraged her every move. "You can do it, Kintana."

The crow's nest, high above her, was a wide, round, slatted platform. She took a deep breath, summoning up more strength, and clambered up another couple of rungs. Kintana couldn't believe how many there were to be mastered, marvelling at the agility of pirates who could run up the ladder like monkeys.

A few more rungs, and the ratlines were rubbing her skin. Her legs were feeling tired too, her muscles aching from gripping with her feet. She fought the urge to look down, trying not to imagine how it would feel to fall from this point. Kintana was beginning to feel lightheaded and she was worried she was going to faint. *Push up*, she told herself.

Polly fluttered at her side. "You're doing great – and I should know I'm a greater vasa parrot!"

Kintana giggled and grabbed the next rung, pulling herself up again; it was getting colder. She looked forward and could see a good distance ahead.

Polly squawked, "Lovely view, isn't it? Wait till you get to the top."

She looked up again at the crow's nest. "I hope it's safe."

"Don't worry, that platform could hold three Pots it's that strong, I promise you."

Kintana conquered the final rungs, then clambered into the crow's nest. She collapsed on to the floor, with relief. The wood seemed sturdy, but she didn't like the little gaps between each slat, nor the open sides. It was like being in a broken laundry tub. She took out Pa's spyglass and looked out to sea, past the ship's bow and its brightly painted figurehead of a seahorse.

Polly perched beside her. "It's breathtaking," Kintana said, "and I don't just mean the climb up!"

"So, how do you like seeing the world from my point of view?" asked Polly, stretching out his wings for preening.

"It's incredible!" Kintana replied, putting away the spyglass. It was strange having a conversation with an animal, but it was nice too – like making a friend. "Everything looks so small. *The Nine Sails* is like a toy ship from up here. Look at those tiny cannons, and the rope looks like thread."

"One thing's for sure, Kintana. You'll never be afraid of heights again after this!"

Kintana checked her hat was snug. "I'll still be glad to get my feet back on the ground. I'll leave the skies for you, Polly."

"That's the way it should be. Imagine if man could fly like birds!"

"Don't worry, that'll never happen," said Kintana, "not unless we suddenly sprout wings! Now, I need to find the *skeleton in the nest*!"

She wrinkled her nose. "Only I don't think there's anything up here." She looked down at the slatted floor. "Oh, wait. I'm wrong. There is something!" She picked up a large piece of black cloth.

Polly stabbed at it with his beak. "It's not food." He scraped it with his talons.

"Careful! Oh no! You've ripped it." Kintana picked up the material, luckily only the edge was torn off. "It's a flag!" she declared, unfolding it.

The design depicted a skeleton striking a heart with an arrow. "A skeleton in a bird's nest, I've solved the final riddle!"

"The King's Death!" said Polly. "That's the name for that particular flag."

"It's scary!"

"It's meant to be," said Polly. "It's a warning that blood will be spilled when pirates attack!"

Kintana shuddered as she folded the flag, carefully placing the cat o'nine tails and the aye-aye hand inside it.

☠

Having scrambled back down, Kintana dashed across the deck, and almost ran straight into Bartholomew in her excitement.

He was carrying a tray with a silver tureen on it. As he swung out of the way, the lid tottered, and brown juice slopped all down his shirt, just missing Sticky. "Oh no," he wailed. "Gangrene will be furious if he sees the state of me."

Polly landed on the boy's head, "You look a mess!"

"Get off me!" he cried.

"Polly!" scolded Kintana. "Hadn't you better go back to your cage? You don't want Gangrene to see you."

The parrot squawked and flew away.

"Don't worry about a bit of gravy," said Kintana, pulling the blue cravat out of her pocket so he could mop his front. "I've some good news for you!" She reached into her jacket and took out the flag. "I've solved the riddles and found the three objects." She unfolded the black material to reveal the cat o'nine tails and the aye-aye hand.

"Oh! I could kiss you!" he exclaimed. "You are ever so clever!"

Kintana laughed. "Why don't you let me carry the tray, then you can take the objects to Mr Gangrene."

Bartholomew beamed at her. "Brilliant." He offered her the used cravat back.

"It should probably go in the laundry," she said, grinning.

"Ha. You're right. Hopefully it will be my last batch and I'll be back on lookout duties soon, thanks to you!"

"What about this stew, shall I take it to Captain Tortuga, for you?"

He shook his head. "No, this tureen is for Mr Gangrene. The captain has already had his." He lifted the lid and pulled a confused face. "I nearly got them muddled . . . one of them has herbs in it – I thought it was this one, but the captain put me right."

Kintana explained how she had worked out each riddle as she and Bartholomew swapped items. Then they walked to the quartermaster's room.

"You go in first," said Kintana. "We don't want Gangrene suspecting I helped you."

He patted her arm in thanks, then knocked.

"Come in . . ."

Bartholomew pushed open the door, "Mr Gangrene . . . I've completed the riddle challenge. I've brought your objects."

Kintana leaned in closer to eavesdrop. She wished she could see Gangrene's face.

"What! Really!" The quartermaster roared with laughter. "Show me then ..."

Kintana smiled to herself picturing Bartholomew handing then over.

"I can hardly believe my eyes!"

"Can I be lookout again?" asked the boy, hopefully.

"Hmm ... Let me speak to Captain Tortuga. In the meantime, get yourself cleaned up. Is that my stew?"

"Err – yes, sir. I had a bit of an accident, but don't worry Kintana is going to bring it in, now."

Gangrene grunted. "Oh, and don't worry about returnin' these things. I'll put them back for you."

Bartholomew gave her a thumbs up as he passed.

Kintana stepped into the quartermaster's study. Gangrene was sitting behind a large desk covered with maps, sea charts, a compass and backstaff for navigating. Snuffles, his pet jumping rat, was perched on top of a pile of logbooks.

Gangrene opened a drawer and pushed the flag, aye-aye hand and cat o'nine tails quickly inside.

Kintana placed the tureen and a spoon on to the desk.

Gangrene barely looked up as he started to eat. She suddenly felt disappointed that he would never know that she had completed the riddle challenge, not Bartholomew. And there was someone else, she wanted to share her pride with – Pa.

Kintana felt a twinge of homesickness but shook it from her mind.

Chapter Eight

PREPARING FOR BATTLE

KINTANA'S STOMACH RUMBLED IN ANTICIPATION of a good dinner as she went to join the rest of the crew.

The pirates were all sitting on benches either side of a long wooden table which was secured to the ceiling by thick ropes.

Kintana sat down next to Bartholomew, as Pots served up the meal on pewter plates.

"Did Gangrene like the stew?" Bartholomew asked, sitting beside her. His shirt was damp and still stained.

"He was tucking into it, when I left."

"Oh, shush, here he is now . . ."

The men sat up straighter as Gangrene stood over them.

Kintana thought she could see tiny lice hopping around the

quartermaster's wiry, grey hair. She tried not to stare as he took a seat next to her.

The pirates began to reminisce about a feast they'd had months ago, but Gangrene barely seemed to be listening. He kept rubbing his eyes and yawning.

"Gangrene and the captain always get much better food," whispered Bartholomew. "You should smell some of the spices Pots uses in Tortuga's meals *and* he gets roast chicken and boiled zebu!" He jabbed his fork in something grey. "Who knows what this is! Squid?"

Kintana giggled, despite herself. "I think it's salt with a sprinkling of boiled vegetables."

"Vegetables? I think this could only be described accurately as mush. Salty mush."

Still I'm so hungry, I'd eat anything, she thought.

Around her, pirates of all shapes, sizes and smells stuffed their faces, the pork mush dripping over unkempt beards and unwashed shirts. She wondered what the collective noun for pirates was – a stink of pirates seemed like a good suggestion, because they all smelled like they needed a bath.

Most of them had their pets with them too, so there was a distinct animal aroma around the table which swung gently with the motion of the ship.

Talk soon turned to battles. Zachariah - a pirate with a fantastic moustache and a green chameleon on his right shoulder - was retelling how he'd lost his arm.

"*The Nine Sails* was under attack from a naval ship. They were firing cannons at us and we were launching twice as many back. I was reloading when the worst blast hit. I don't remember much about it, tell the truth, and thank 'eavens for that."

"That must have been some pain you were in," said Bartholomew, as Sticky tickled his neck with his orange antennae. "A cannon ball would knock your arm clear off!"

Kintana smothered her giggles, as the other pirates laughed – only Gangrene didn't join in. His head has slumped into his chest.

The dokotera slapped his own forehead in disbelief. "Aah, Bartholomew, I can tell you're a landlubber. It's not the cannon ball that does the damage. When one of them things collides with your ship, there's bits of wood flyin' all over the place. Get a big splinter wedged in your leg, then next thing you know your foot has turned green, and they have to chop it off. If that doesn't work, the badness spreads and soon enough you drop down dead."

Bartholomew turned the colour of his dinner. "Oh, I see." He pushed his plate away.

"I hope we get through tomorrow's battle without too many injuries," said Croak.

"Well, let's hope they surrender as soon as they see our flag," whispered Zachariah, wiping tack crumbs from his moustache.

Croak jabbed him with an elbow. "I was talkin', Zachariah . . . anyway, the dokotera will do his best to fix us up, won't you Spike," he nodded at the man with the spiky hair and a pet tenrec.

Gangrene jerked awake. "Err, who, whatcha." He had drooled down his chin. He wiped away the spittle and frowned.

Kintana chomped on a hardtack biscuit. *What is wrong with the quartermaster? Is he ill?* she wondered.

"When the grappling hooks are secure, we roar like animals," said Pots. "We scream and shout all sorts of threats at the other men, until their knees tremble. A bit of cutlass-waving, or a few shots fired into the air, secures their defeat. We rarely do any actual fighting. They surrender quick enough, after all, they don't own the loot on board, they're only transporting it. But if they won't give up without a fight, then so be it."

"Poor Bartholomew, we all know how accident prone you are," said Spike. "Don't fret, we have an insurance scheme for injuries!"

"He'll be all right," said Zachariah, as his chameleon shot out its tongue at a fly. "He's so skinny, all he needs to do is stand behind Pots. The cannon balls will bounce right off 'is belly!"

"Hey!" said Pots.

Gangrene was scowling at the cook. His eyes widened in sudden revelation. "You did tell Bartholomew which stew was for the captain, didn't you? You didn't decide to switch them?"

"Of course not."

He knit his eyebrows. "What about you, Spotty. Did you make another of your mistakes?"

"No, sir."

"Because if either of you have been playin' tricks," Gangrene waved his finger. "There'll be hell to pay." He stumbled to his feet. "I need some fresh air."

"Aye, we should all get back to our duties," said Croak. "There's lots of work to be done, before we are ready for our next attack."

Kintana's stomach felt funny again, not from hunger but from anxiety.

"You look like you need some fresh air too, young Kintana?" said Gangrene. "Come, let's go up on deck."

She stood up, put her hat back on, and followed him outside. The sun was slowly setting on a long day – and her old life.

"Enjoyin' life on board?" asked Gangrene, stifling another yawn. "All that talk of battles got your blood pumpin'?"

"Hmm," she replied. "I've always wanted to be a pirate."

"You know, you remind me a lot of me as a lad. I must have been your age when I went to sea," he said. "I know exactly how you are feelin'. Excited. Apprehensive. I remember, being on my first ship and lookin' up at the stars and feelin' so small."

Kintana gazed at the vast sky. Actually, it made her feel the opposite, she felt a strength now that she could do anything. Gangrene was watching her, and a surprising thought entered her head – that somehow, he'd known exactly how she'd feel.

"You'll make a great pirate," he said, rubbing his eyes again. "You'll be unstoppable!"

Kintana wanted to believe him. She tried to picture herself wielding a cutlass. "I might need a few lessons in combat . . ."

"Not a problem. To be honest, hand-to-hand fightin' is a last resort. We've got cannons and muskets, and home-made bombs to take the wind out of the enemy," said Gangrene. "And a little smoke always helps with confusin' the other crew. If anyone survives that and gets too close that's when we use blades and flintlock pistols." He flashed his weapons that were tucked into his belt: "We can be very persuasive in gettin' our targets to hand over their cargo."

Gangrene stretched his arms, in one final, noisy yawn. "There could be real booty – jewels, ivory, silver, fancy furs or even gold! Hopefully, there'll be some good food and drink too! Even though you're only a boy, you still get a half share."

Kintana brimmed with excitement, picturing herself surrounded by piles of treasure! There might be diamonds. Rubies. Emeralds. Pa wouldn't believe it, if she returned home loaded up with jewels!

Chapter Nine

WALKING THE PLANK

THE DAYS PASSED WITH A GROWING FAMILIARITY. Kintana worked hard from dawn 'til dusk, she had all the animals to care for and she was getting lessons in cutlass fighting from Gangrene. At the end of each long day, she would go to bed, exhausted, and yet she found it increasingly difficult to sleep.

At first, she thought it was just a case of getting used to a hammock, but every night the same queasy feeling sat in the pit of her stomach. The dokotera said it was probably mild seasickness, but the truth was the further they sailed away from Pirate Island, the more she missed home. When she did finally fall asleep, Kintana kept dreaming she was back at the pet shop, and that Pa was in floods of tears because all the animals had run away.

Pots, in the next hammock along, gave a large, stinky burp. "Ah!" he said. "There's nothing like a raid! Gives you a real appetite. Speaking of which, it's time I was making breakfast."

Kintana rolled over in her hammock and pretended to be asleep. Perhaps he'd let her have a lie-in for once.

No such luck. Pots rocked her hammock. "That means you should be up too, laddie. Shake a leg."

Kintana groaned and reached under her pillow for a stubby tallow candle. First port of call was the ship's heads – two boxes either side of the bowsprit used as a toilet. She lit the candle and placed it in a holder so the melting wax wouldn't drip on to her hand. The flame illuminated the dark oak slats all around with a flickering light.

She pulled her clothes on over her long nightshirt and slipped her shoes on. She wished she could have a wash; she felt sweaty and itchy and her clothes didn't smell very fresh.

As she tiptoed past, the hammocks swayed like spectres possessed by the spirit and motion of the ship. Their occupants slumbered noisily as Kintana avoided their dangling hairy, tattooed arms.

The cramped corridor smelled of stale sweat and green spit mixed with salty, sodden wood and she was glad to get outside.

☠

After using the toilet, Kintana went back down to the galley; she greeted Whiskers – who was curled up under the table – and began to peel and chop the vegetables.

Pots waved a ladle about as though it was a cutlass. "Won't be long now," he cried.

There was a commotion at the door as Gangrene stormed into the room. "Where's that boy?"

Kintana recoiled. *Does he mean me?*

"I'm gonna throttle that Bartholomew!"

She sighed with relief.

Pots's fossa was pacing up and down.

"What's Pimples done now?" asked Pots, rolling his eye.

"Later . . . Have you seen him?"

Pots shook his head.

"What about you, have you seen him?" he stared at Kintana.

"No, Mr Gangrene."

He snarled and staggered away. "I'll make him walk Plank."

"Come on," said Pots, "I want to see this . . ."

Walk the plank? Kintana gulped. *Oh no!* She imagined Bartholomew blindfolded being shunted along a piece of wood and then shoved off the end into the icy depths.

She hurried after the cook.

Gangrene's shouting brought dozens of pirates on to deck including Captain Tortuga, who was standing with his arms akimbo.

Bartholomew cowered next to him. Sticky clung on to the boy's collar, his antennae exploring the air. The boy's shirt was damp from doing the laundry, Kintana couldn't help thinking he was about to look a lot wetter. "What have I done," he squeaked.

Gangrene narrowed his eyes. "You know what you did." He pulled back his waistcoat to reveal his shirt – the once pristine white material was now streaked with reddish pink.

"Oh, that . . ." said Bartholomew. "It wasn't my fault! Honest! Somehow a red bandana got in with all the whites . . ."

Captain Tortuga sighed. "Have you decided on an appropriate punishment?"

"I have." A wicked smile spread across Gangrene's face. "I want him to walk Plank."

The pirates murmured. "Not Plank," one whispered. "That's too cruel," agreed another. "He's only a boy," said a third, "he'll never manage it."

Kintana chewed her thumb, nervously, as Gangrene shoved a trembling Bartholomew towards the side of the ship. She looked round for a piece of timber, but couldn't see one, only a large pile of straw.

She snuck closer. Now she could see a long piece of rope was sticking out.

Gangrene took hold of the end and passed it to a sobbing Bartholomew.

"I can't do it," he wept. "I'm not strong enough."

"You can and you will," snarled the quartermaster.

Bartholomew grumbled and placed the rope over his shoulder and began to pull.

He groaned with effort.

Kintana was confused. *What is he trying to do? Is the rope attached to a heavy plank?*

"Someone, help," he moaned, pulling harder, beads of sweat on his forehead.

Gangrene huffed. "He's even weaker than I thought. We'll be here all day . . ."

"Kintana, see if you can get Plank to move," said Captain Tortuga.

She ran towards the dome of straw and pushed her hands into the mound, spreading her fingers over something hard and smooth.

Kintana started to sweep away the golden stalks, catching a glimpse of thick scaly skin as the animal underneath stirred. She lifted off big clumps of straw now, tossing it to one side. She could see the top of the animal's carapace. The shell was huge! She worked faster, feeling giddy. *Is Plank a tortoise? A giant tortoise?*

Almost in answer the herbivore poked out his grey head.

He is! She beamed. *Bartholomew's punishment isn't to walk off a plank into the sea, he has to walk the world's biggest, slowest tortoise!*

"Well done, Kintana," said Pots. "Now, Captain, won't you tell Pimples here to take the beast for a one way walk to my galley. He'd make a fine dinner for us all!"

Kintana gasped. "You wouldn't really eat him?"

Captain Tortuga patted Plank's head, "Well, I must admit, I did buy him as emergency rations."

"Best use for him," muttered Gangrene. "Tortoise meat is supposed to be sweet and fatty. They swear there's no finer taste than its liver, cooked in its own oil."

"No!" cried Kintana, "You can't eat him! Look at his face!" Plank stretched his neck to investigate her. She stroked the top of his soft, warm head. "It's all right boy. I'll protect you."

Chapter Ten

HOIST THE FLAG

CAPTAIN TORTUGA BENT DOWN AND HUGGED his reptile. "Don't fret, young Kintana. Although these island tortoises are sold as portable dinners, I've grown rather attached to Plank. There's no way I would eat him now! It was Mr Gangrene's idea that giving him exercise could be used as a punishment."

Kintana smiled. "I don't think walking him is a punishment! I would love to do it. Giant tortoises are amazing creatures, I've heard they can live over 100 years, maybe even 200!"

"Great," muttered Gangrene. "It'll outlive the lot of us."

"Wouldn't that be something!" exclaimed Tortuga. "I've been studying him to see if I can work out his secret of longevity. I would like to know how they reproduce too. I had hoped to find another one on Nosy Boraha."

"Oh, aye, let's get a shipful," said Gangrene, shaking his head.

"Sadly, finding Plank a mate has proved impossible. It seems there are no other surviving Madagascar giant tortoises."

Kintana thought that was awful if it was true.

She watched Bartholomew start to slowly walk Plank round the deck – then made her way back to the ship's galley. She still had the animals to feed.

"How come Plank isn't on my list," she asked the cook.

"Isn't he? The captain's always giving him treats, so he wouldn't have starved. But you can give him extra cabbage today if it makes you feel better."

She added some to her tray and set off on her rounds.

☠

An hour later, she returned to the galley to help Pots with the crew's breakfast. He pointed to a large wooden tub. "There's oats in there, we'll need a good thirty scoops in the big pan with plenty of water."

Kintana did as she was told.

"Add a bit of salt, then keep stirring the porridge."

The shelves were filled with jars and bottles, but it was too dark to read the labels to know if they contained the salt she needed. She reached out to look at each in turn. The fossa hissed.

Pots span round, "All right, Whiskers, all right." He patted the animal before reaching up and selecting a jar. "This one's the salt."

Kintana took it, keeping an eye on the fossa, as she sprinkled some into the pan. She gave the porridge a stir; as it slowly warmed.

After a few minutes, the cook nudged her aside and lifted the ladle. "Hmm, it will do," he said. "Right, get the latch, I'm going to take this through to the rest of the crew – you grab some bowls."

Kintana adjusted her hat, then stacked the bowls up and followed the cook through to the berth.

"Breakfast's ready!" called Pots, throwing down the big pan of porridge.

The pirates rubbed their weary eyes and stifled yawns. They'd only had four hours sleep as was usual for shifts.

"Did you hear that strange noise, last night?" asked the dokotera, taking a bowl of porridge from Kintana.

"Like a howl?" Croak nodded. "It was awful. I don't care what the captain says. It *was* Blackbeard!"

"We all know it's 'im," agreed Zachariah, stroking his chameleon. He leaned in and whispered to the men. "When I was down in the 'old, fetching some new sail cloth ... I saw 'im! 'e was 'unched in the shadows!"

"Behave, that howling was probably one of the captain's animals," said Pots.

"He doesn't have any dogs or wolves," said Kintana.

"See! It *is* Blackbeard," Croak insisted, the tomato frog popping up out of his shirt pocket.

"'e considered 'imself invincible," said Zachariah. "A man like that doesn't believe 'e'll ever die."

"But he did die," said Kintana. "He was stabbed in the neck, shot and then had his head lopped off."

"Aye, but does he realise he's dead?" asked Croak. "Spike, isn't it true a chicken can run round after they chop its head off. Could it be the same with Blackbeard?"

The dokotera stared at his porridge. "All I know is that sound was supernatural; it made my hair stand on end!"

"Nonsense," said Pots.

There was a moaning sound from the door.

Everyone's head turned as one.

"It's him!" said Croak.

Kintana cringed. She could hear footsteps coming nearer.

The tomato frog hid in Croak's pocket and Spike's tenrec shivered. Even Zachariah's chameleon closed its eyes.

Thud, thud, thud.

Even Pots look nervous.

The moaning was louder. The spectre's shadow appeared in the doorway.

It was strangely long and thin for the infamous Blackbeard.

"Bartholomew! Oh!" The pirates all cursed him.

The boy's hair was more unruly than ever, and he had dark shadows under his eyes. "I'm exhausted," he complained. "I never want to walk Plank ever again."

Even Sticky looked limper than normal. He peeled the insect off his lapel and placed him lovingly on the table.

"I'll get you some porridge," said Kintana, jumping up.

Bartholomew slumped on to the bench.

She thrust a bowl in front of him, just as the ship reeled, and he fell forward, his face plopping down into his breakfast.

"Best wash it down with a drink," said Pots, grabbing a pewter tankard and throwing cold water over Bartholomew.

"*Urrghh!* What did you do that for?" he cried, wiping wet slop from his face.

"To try and wake you up," said Pots. "But then you're always half asleep aren't you. I've never met anyone as dozy as you!"

Oh dear, thought Kintana. *Why is he always getting himself in trouble?*

☠

Bartholomew's misfortune turned out to be Kintana's good luck.

"It seems we need a temporary lookout, after all," said Gangrene that afternoon. "If you still fancy the job."

"Really?" she glowed with excitement. "Of course."

"Excellent." Gangrene slapped her on the shoulder. "I can't risk sendin' Bartholomew up, can I? He's likely to fall to his death."

The crew all gathered round Captain Tortuga. "I want everything ready for when we get the word from Kintana. Down to the magazine, men. I want those cannons loaded."

Kintana checked for Pa's brass spyglass in her pocket, and crossed to the rigging, feeling much more confident about climbing the ratlines this time.

Once she'd reached the top of the main mast, she clambered into the crow's nest and put Pa's spyglass to her eye. She followed the line of the horizon.

There was something moving in the distance. She panned the spyglass. "Ship ahoy!" she hollered, pointing.

"Well done, lad," called Gangrene.

"Prepare to hoist the flag!" bellowed Captain Tortuga.

"Yes, Captain!"

Kintana bent down to attach the flag to the pole.

The wooden slats were bare. Her heart gave a thud with anxiety. The flag wasn't there.

Coldness plunged in Kintana's stomach. *Why hasn't Gangrene put it back?*

"It's not here," she called, her voice breaking.

"It must be," shouted Gangrene. "Look again."

She did as instructed though she knew it was pointless. All she found was a small scrap of black material. It must have fallen off when Polly accidentally tore the corner with his talons.

Kintana pushed it into her jacket pocket and scrambled back down the rigging.

More of the crew were gathering below the crow's nest – Croak, Spike, Zachariah, and Pots all stood round, whispering in each other's ears.

"Fetch Bartholomew," demanded Captain Tortuga.

☠

Kintana had reached the deck. "Could the flag be somewhere else?" She tried to read Gangrene's face.

"Such as?" he asked, cocking his head to one side.

She shrugged.

There was silence while they waited for Bartholomew.

The boy looked utterly devastated when he finally appeared.

"Blackbeard's ghost must have stolen the flag," Bartholomew rambled. "I told you he was haunting the ship, but you wouldn't believe me."

"Idiot," said Gangrene.

But the rest of the crew were nodding in agreement.

"What if the boy's right?" asked Zachariah. "What if there is a Captain's Curse!"

"Blackbeard will be stabbing us in our beds next, wait and see," added Croak, his face redder than ever.

"There is *NO* such thing as curses," shouted Tortuga. "If the flag has gone, someone here knows where it went."

Kintana realised Gangrene wasn't going to say anything about the riddle challenge – and neither was Bartholomew.

I could tell Captain Tortuga that I took the flag, but what if Gangrene denies any part in it? She knew the captain would believe his loyal quartermaster over a new cabin boy.

And if she confessed, and the captain did believe her, he would punish her for sure. He might even whip her with the cat o'nine tails, if she admitted she'd taken that too. But if she said nothing, then Bartholomew would be punished, and he was already in trouble.

Kintana didn't know what to do.

Chapter Eleven

REVELATIONS

"**W**ELL, THERE GOES OUR SHARE OF ANY BOOTY," groaned Spike. "If we can't hoist the flag, we can't attack the merchant ship. Not without a full out battle."

"First, we lose Eyeball, *now* the flag is missing," mumbled Croak. "It is a curse."

"Captain," said Pots, firmly. "You promised us treasure galore but that ship also meant fresh supplies. With all these animals on board we need more food."

Gangrene raised his hand. "Hold on there, Pots! I'm sure Captain Tortuga has another plan up his sleeve. Let's not be hasty. We wouldn't want a mutiny."

Kintana gasped. Would the pirates really rebel against their captain?

"We all voted for Tortuga to be in charge . . ." added the

quartermaster.

"That's true," said Zachariah. "But look at the situation we're in."

Pots nodded. "Perhaps we should consider replacing him." He turned to face the rest of the crew and ran a finger discreetly across his own throat.

Kintana's eyes widened in shock.

The rest of the crew were closing in, forming a tightening circle like a hangman's noose.

"We can still take the ship," insisted Tortuga. "We've plenty of gunpowder, cutlasses and cannon balls."

"Enough for twenty battles, Captain," agreed Gangrene. "And I'm sure the men are ready to fight – to the death, if need be!"

Kintana's stomach churned.

"*You* might be," said Croak. "The rest of us want to avoid fighting and not just to save our necks! We don't want all that treasure and food shot to pieces or sunk to the bottom of the ocean!"

Bartholomew began to wail. "We're all going to die! We're all going to die!"

"Shut up!" ordered Tortuga. "WE ARE NOT!"

"Well, chances are, some of us will," said Gangrene, cocking his head towards Bartholomew.

"But I don't want to die!"

"To be fair, this is your fault," said Gangrene. "You've messed up bein' lookout. You've messed up hoistin' the flag. No doubt you'll start firin' cannon balls into our own hull next."

"It's not my fault!" Bartholomew wept. "It's . . . it's . . ." He pointed at Kintana. "Her's!"

Kintana gulped.

All the pirates were staring at her. They looked very, very angry.

"*Her's*?" said Tortuga. "Bartholomew. Are you saying Kintana is a girl?"

She gasped. How did he know?

"Obviously Kintana's a girl, look at the way she wears a lamba, look at her hair! I might be stupid, but I'm not blind! Besides Kintana is a girl's name."

Gangrene stared at Kintana. "Are you a girl?"

She nodded.

"Oh!" moaned Zachariah. "That's why everything's going wrong!"

"A girl on *The Nine Sails*!" cried Croak. "We're doomed!"

"Kintana is the reason for all our bad luck!" said Pots.

"Stop," said Bartholomew, "I didn't mean you to blame Kintana for all our troubles, only for the flag . . . listen it's the Captain's Curse – I know it is."

No one was listening.

"Dokotera, did *you* know Kintana was a girl?" asked Gangrene.

Spike shrugged. "Sure. I just presumed the captain was fine with having girl pirates on board, after all it is the 18th century!"

The other pirates groaned.

"Shall I tie the girl to the mast for a flogging, Captain?" continued Pots.

"I can fetch the cat o'nine tails," offered Gangrene.

"Flogging is too good for her. I say we give her a dunking then throw her overboard for the sharks," said the pirate with the coua.

"Keelhaul her," shouted another. "The hull barnacles will rip her to shreds!"

Captain Tortuga held up his hand. "Enough! I am still in charge and that means I decide on the punishment!" He grabbed Kintana by the arm and dragged her away.

"Ow! You're hurting me."

Bartholomew rushed after them. "Captain, what are you going to do to her?"

"I haven't decided yet."

"Please," begged Kintana. "Please, this is not my fault. You had bad luck onboard long before I arrived."

"That's true, it's because of the Captain's Curse," said Bartholomew. "Captain, I'm telling you!"

"You're telling me?!" The captain pulled off his hat and threw it at the boy. His bald head was dripping with sweat. He grabbed the boy's arm. "You will come with me too."

He stormed across the deck, pulling Kintana and Bartholomew along. "Never mind gawping, the rest of you . . . FIND. THAT. FLAG!"

☠

Tortuga kicked open the door to his cabin. Polly squawked from his cage on the captain's desk. "What's all the commotion?"

"A girl!" Tortuga repeated. "On MY ship!"

"Oh, is that what all the noise is about?" asked Polly, rolling his eyes. "It's not *Kintana* you should be worried about, Captain. Gangrene's playing you for a fool!"

"*What* did you say?" Tortuga stared at the vasa parrot.

"You're being set up." Polly flapped his wings.

The captain stared at the parrot. "Am I? Talk, bird!"

Kintana's heart was still racing.

"I think Gangrene had the flag stolen on purpose," said Polly, calmly. "He wants to take over as captain."

61

"That's nonsense," insisted Tortuga. "Mr Gangrene is my second in command. He's my most loyal crew member. He was the only one of the crew to speak up for me."

"It's not Gangrene. It's not Kintana. It's Blackbeard's ghost!" moaned Bartholomew.

"If you don't shut up, I'll tie *you* to the mast with her. You'll *both* get fifty lashes! Where's my cat o'nine tails?"

Polly gave a long whistle.

The captain slumped into his chair. "How am I supposed to go into battle when my crew have lost all respect for me? How could this happen? How have things changed so quickly?"

Is Polly right? Is this a plot by Gangrene – and perhaps Pots – to take over the ship?!

This wasn't the time to confess her part in the flag's disappearance, but she had to do something.

Kintana's mouth was dry with nerves. "I might know how to find the flag . . ."

Chapter Twelve

SNIFFING OUT
THE TRUTH

TORTUGA GAVE KINTANA A HARD STARE. "YOU might know how to find the flag?"

She nodded and pulled out the torn piece of flag from her pocket. "I found this when I was in the crow's nest. We could get Mr Gangrene's pet, Snuffles, to smell it and find the rest of it!"

"Hmm," Tortuga nodded. "Giant jumping rats have an excellent sense of smell. It might work."

"Shall I fetch him?" she asked. "While the pirates start looking."

The captain narrowed his eyes. "Be quick."

"Yes, Captain," Kintana replied and rushed to the galley.

She could hear Pots and Gangrene arguing below. So, she crept down the stairs and paused at the door, placing her ear to the wood.

The cook was trying to soothe a hissing Whiskers between apologies to the quartermaster.

"Get that mangy cat in her crate," barked Gangrene, "She's almost torn my arm off!"

"It's just a scratch," spat Pots. "She was only acting guard."

"I know that," he snapped, "but she's not supposed to attack me."

"It's not Whiskers's fault; she can smell Snuffles on you. She's a hunter."

"Well, this is your last warning. If she comes near me again, I'll throw her overboard."

"You're not to touch her. Anyway, she's looking after *him*, isn't she?"

"Him?" repeated Kintana. *Did they have someone hidden in the galley? A stowaway?*

"Lookin' after him!" jeered Gangrene. "Whiskers nearly knocked the jar onto the floor . . . It *is* still in one piece, isn't it?"

"I told you it was. If you don't trust me, I'll show you."

Kintana still had no idea what they were arguing about. She could hear Gangrene tapping his foot.

"Go on then."

There was a scraping and rustling sound.

"See," said Pots. "No damage done."

"Hmm. Not this time. Still, I want you to keep that creature of yours out of my way or I might be tempted to feed her a portion of your special stew!"

"Look, it's not my fault Bartholomew got the tureens mixed up. The boy's so stupid! I still can't believe he actually got you the flag!"

"Neither can I!" agreed Gangrene. "Still, I wish he would

shut up about the Captain's Curse. The ghost stories were only supposed to frighten the crew to stop them snoopin' about."

Kintana took a deep breath, then made loud fake footsteps as though she was just coming below decks, calling out, "Mr Gangrene."

She pushed open the door. "The captain needs you!"

He looked surprised. "Still with us? I thought you'd be swimmin' home!"

"I'm not that easy to get rid of," Kintana replied.

☠

Gangrene stood in front of Captain Tortuga. "You wanted me, sir?"

"Actually, I want your giant jumping rat." He smiled at Kintana.

"Snuffles? What do you want him for? Nobody touches my baby, except me."

"Captain's orders, Mr Gangrene. I need your pet to find the flag. Kintana made an excellent observation that your giant jumping rat could sniff it out."

The quartermaster curled his lip. "She did, did she?" He shot her a dirty look.

"Hand him over . . ."

"Yes, Captain." Gangrene pulled Snuffles out from inside his shirt.

"I have a scrap of flag here for him to sniff," said Tortuga.

"Really?" He seemed more annoyed than surprised.

The captain held the piece of material in front of Snuffles's nose.

Kintana grinned as the giant jumping rat took in the scent.

"Daddy needs you to find somethin'" said Gangrene. "Find the flag, Snuffles, find the flag."

He placed his pet onto the ground. Snuffles sat on his back legs, his front paws twitching near his nose. Kintana thought he looked ever so cute.

"He's got the scent!" exclaimed Tortuga.

The giant jumping rat was off, leaping along the deck and down towards the berth. The captain and Gangrene sprinted after him. Kintana at their heels.

Why isn't he heading to Gangrene's cabin? Surely that's where he's hidden the flag?

Had she made a mistake?

Snuffles leapt along the hammocks scurrying over sleeping pirates.

"He's gettin' closer, see? He's all excited," said Gangrene.

His pet had reached Bartholomew's hammock. He stopped and began to dig.

"He's found something!" Gangrene pulled back the woollen blanket revealing the missing flag. "It was the boy all along!" He gave a sly grin. "I'll bring the miscreant to your cabin!"

Kintana opened her mouth to object.

Gangrene wagged his finger. "Don't be silly. This is nothin' to do with you."

She clenched her fists in frustration.

☠

Hours passed before Kintana felt it was safe enough to take food to the captain's animals.

Tortuga was up on deck, so she was safe to speak to Polly while she saw to his collection. She let the parrot out and he perched on top of his cage. She gave a bowl of worms to a tenrec and a dish of cockroaches to a chameleon.

"They've tied Bartholomew up in the hold," Kintana told him, taking off her hat. "There's going to be a trial."

"But Bartholomew didn't take the flag," squawked Polly. "We did."

"Do you think I should tell Tortuga the truth." She ran her fingers along the soft felt. Pa would know what to do. "Should I speak out at the hearing?"

"I don't think the captain would believe you. He'll only think you're trying to save your friend."

"I suppose."

"Did they say where they're going to hold the trial?"

Kintana nodded. She'd had mixed feelings when she'd heard. "Tortuga is turning *The Nine Sails* around. We're going back to Pirate Island."

"Well at least there's a chance I can escape this ship," said Polly. "I don't want to end up at the bottom of the sea like Eyeball."

"The navigator?" asked Kintana, putting her hat back on. "Do you know something about the accident?"

"No! How could I? I was in my cage." Polly suddenly flapped his wings. "You're trying to trick me! Eyeball was crazy that's why he fell overboard, he definitely wasn't pushed."

"*Pushed*?"

"I said NOT pushed!"

"You have to tell me the truth, Polly. Did you see Eyeball that night?"

The parrot was frantic. Hopping up and down.

"Don't be afraid . . ." she gently stroked his head.

Polly sighed. "Eyeball was covered in scratches. He was delirious too. He was ranting about being attacked by mad monkeys. He said he'd found Kidd's treasure. That he was going to be rich!"

She stepped back. "Mad monkeys? Do you mean lemurs? There are no monkeys on Pirate Island . . ."

"I don't know, I guess so." He tucked his head under his wing. "Everyone said Eyeball had sunstroke or had drunk too much grog. Only Gangrene seemed to have any sympathy for him. He took Eyeball out on deck to get some fresh air."

"So, you did see them!"

"I was flying around the crow's nest when I heard lots of shouting down on the deck . . .. I couldn't really see clearly, but a few minutes later I heard – SPLASH!" Polly straightened up. "Eyeball was gone. I swooped down to see what had happened, and that's when Gangrene grabbed me. He gave me to the captain, and I've been trapped in that cage ever since."

"How awful!" said Kintana.

"I reckon Gangrene wants the treasure for himself."

"My pa told me about all the captains," she said, dishing out the rest of the food. "Didn't Kidd's ship get sunk at Pirate Island years ago?"

"That's right," agreed Polly. "I guess that's why the rumours started about him burying his treasure on Nosy Boraha. William Kidd was a complicated man. He was paid to catch pirates, they nicknamed him The Pirate Hunter. Only it turned out Kidd wasn't much different to the pirates he hunted – he certainly liked to hold onto confiscated booty."

"What happened?"

"The authorities captured him, accused him of being a pirate, and put him on trial in London. Kidd insisted he was innocent. No one knows what happened to all the treasure he'd kept for himself. Some of the witnesses said he'd buried it on Nosy Boraha, that he'd left a series of clues as to its whereabouts, so he could find it when he returned to the island. Only, he never got the chance."

"They found him guilty?"

"Yes, he was executed—"

There was a noise in the room next door. "The captain's back," said Kintana. "I'd better get going . . ."

"Shhh, wait," said Polly, putting out his wing to stop her. "That's not Tortuga. I'd recognise that stink anywhere – it's Gangrene and his giant jumping rat."

Kintana peered round the heavy drape. Polly hopped on to her shoulder and tried to see too.

Gangrene was rummaging in the captain's drawer.

Is he putting the cat o'nine tails and aye-aye finger back?

No. He was taking something out.

"He's got a book," she whispered, "But I can't see which one."

"It's probably an ABC."

"It might be important! I'll have to sneak into Gangrene's room, next time he's out, and find it," said Kintana.

Chapter Thirteen

DROP ANCHOR

KINTANA TRIED TO STAY POSITIVE ON BOARD *The Nine Sails* in the days following Bartholomew's containment, but it was difficult. As the ship made its way back to the island, she did her best to sneak into Gangrene's room, but it was either locked or occupied. When she did go in to speak to him on some pretence or other, he told her he was busy and sent her away.

She decided to clear her mind by taking Polly on deck for some fresh air, although she had to keep him in his cage. The ship's masts and yard arms creaked overhead like an old man breathing in and out.

Excitement and nerves stirred in her stomach as Tortuga steered *The Nine Sails* up the channel between Nosy Boraha and Madagascar, towards Pirate Island.

Kintana licked her lips; the saltiness that was constantly

in the air had made her mouth sore and dry, and the taste only emphasised her thirst. The crew were all on grog – a disgusting mixture of stale, green water mixed with rum. She screwed up her face whenever she saw a pirate sipping it, gnashers gritted to sift out the algae! It was no wonder their teeth fell out and tongues swelled – and many had serious stomach and toilet problems! The smells were worse than the sulphur stink bombs some of the pirates were fond of making.

Pots had banned Kintana from the galley now everyone knew she was a girl. She'd even offered to look after Whiskers, but the cook just shooed her away. She was lucky Captain Tortuga had decided to allow her to return home rather than marooning her.

Polly was swinging upside-down from his perch.

"What do you know about Pots?" Kintana asked.

"Not much, except he used to work for Blackbeard – he was cook on board *The Adventure*." Polly replied. "Then he got a job with Tortuga. There's hardly any of the famous captains still alive; I reckon the golden age of piracy is over."

"Ahoy!" called a voice from high up in the crow's nest. "Pirate Island straight ahead."

Polly squawked with delight. Kintana had promised to let him go if it was safe to do so.

"Shush," she urged.

"Sorry! It's just, I can't wait to fly home to beautiful Nosy Boraha. I bet poor Bartholomew's not looking forward to our arrival though."

"What will happen to him?" Kintana asked.

"He'll be held at the old fort on Nosy Boraha. It is well guarded, and they don't allow visitors. All the pirates will be given the opportunity to speak at his trial, though you can guarantee they will have nothing of importance to say. Those that don't want to give evidence will no doubt spend their shore leave digging holes trying to find Captain Kidd's treasure. Nosy Boraha must have more holes than a family of mice."

"Shouldn't be long till we dock if this wind keeps up," said Kintana.

Polly gave a squawk. "Oh no, here comes Gangrene and the captain. Hide me!"

Kintana tucked behind a couple of barrels so she could eavesdrop. She wanted to know what the quartermaster was saying.

The captain wiped his bald head. "I want to get this trial over and done with. Then we can continue on our original route."

"Understood, Captain," replied Gangrene, squirming as Snuffles stuck his head out of his shirt. The giant jumping rat's nose twitched rapidly.

Suddenly Snuffles leapt out and scurried towards the galley ventilation grill in the centre of the deck.

"Come back, baby!" cried Gangrene.

Kintana was expecting Snuffles to disappear through the wooden lattice, but at the last moment the giant jumping rat halted.

Down below, Whiskers hissed. Snuffles's nose was twitching more than ever.

Surely Snuffles won't go near the fossa. They eat giant jumping rats!

Gangrene ran over to Snuffles and scooped him up. "Thank the stars!" He kissed the top of his pet's head over and over. "Daddy's got you. You're safe now." Then he tucked Snuffles back into the top of his shirt.

"You should take more care of your animal," said Tortuga.

"He must be hungry," said Gangrene. "He knows not to go in the galley. I'd better take him back to my quarters and feed him. Sorry, Captain."

☠

The Nine Sails was preparing to drop anchor at Pirate Island's harbour and the crew were all in good spirits.

"I can almost taste coconut in the air!" proclaimed Croak as Kintana lifted Polly's cage on to the top of a barrel and prepared for going ashore.

"I can't wait to get a drink of good clean water," said the dokotera.

"Never mind water I want some rum!" added Zachariah.

Kintana sighed; the island was beautiful. She felt comforted by the familiar white sand, lush green grass, tall palms, and banana plants along the coast.

Malagasy fishermen cast their nets from brightly painted boats – wooden dugouts that bobbed with the tide. Their families helped transport their catch, little children with their fingers under the gills of long eels and fresh fish.

Being back made her realise more than ever how much she had missed Pirate Island.

"It's good to be home," said Polly, echoing her thoughts.

Kintana leaned over the ship's side. The sea was a perfect green-blue, little fish were swimming around. "It is."

The calm was destroyed by a ruckus on deck. She turned to see Bartholomew – his hands and legs were in irons and Captain Tortuga was forcing him across the deck. The boy looked dishevelled and exhausted. Sticky, his giant stick insect was limp and pale on his lapel.

Gangrene and Pots stood guard. The quartermaster had a tight grip on Snuffles. There was no sign of Whiskers, however. The fossa must be staying behind in the galley.

Kintana looked up at the fort, where they were going to take Bartholomew. She'd never been up close to the old building, but she could imagine it was cold and damp and dark inside the dungeon. She shuddered. It was her fault he was being taken to the old fort. She'd taken the flag, not him.

She turned to the other pirates, who were gathering at her side, waiting to cross to Pirate Island too.

"What happens if Bartholomew is found guilty?" Kintana asked them, afraid to hear the answer.

"They'll hang him and bury him in the pirate cemetery," said Croak, sadly.

She recoiled in horror. "I can't let that happen! I have to give evidence!"

"Only pirates can speak at the trial," said Spike, "and you're not one any more. Besides, you don't want to go muddying the waters. Tortuga and Gangrene are already cross with you. One wrong word and they might lock you up in the old fort too."

"Take my advice and go 'ome, little girl," added Zachariah.

Kintana sighed, checked her hat, and picked up her knapsack, as the gangplank was lowered. Then she swiftly undid the catch on Polly's cage.

The parrot began to sing.

> "Watch where you sail to, my boy.
> There's trouble ahead
> Hold on to your wig
> And don't lose your head ..."

Kintana giggled. The parrot seemed so happy, and his antics soon made her forget her own worries. She opened the cage door and watched as he soared away.

Chapter Fourteen

HO, HO, HO AND A BOTTLE OF RUM

BACK ON LAND, KINTANA MADE HER WAY ALONG the harbour to the stockade. Then through the gates, passing the familiar wooden huts on stilts. She could see the pet shop with its swinging sign and banana leaf roof.

"I should tell Pa I'm back. He'll be surprised to see me again so soon." *Pleased, too*, she thought.

She ran across to the shop and flung open the door. "Pa! It's me! I'm home!"

There was no reply. No sign of Pa. She searched the shop, the kitchen, and their bedrooms.

Kintana shook her head; she knew where he would probably be. She checked the pets had enough food and fresh water, then gathered up her things and headed to the tavern.

Although it was mid-afternoon, the Leaky Boat tavern was fit to bursting. The pub was packed with pirates.

Kintana pushed open the wooden door and stepped inside to the sound of an accordion, wheezing out a melancholy song.

The musician was standing tucked into one of the inn's many corners. The place was like a rabbit warren, made up of a series of darkened rooms with low ceilings decorated with the most basic of seating, old barrels and an abundance of sawdust. The old pirate began to accompany his playing; singing of his miseries at sea, including how he'd lost several of his teeth and all of his money on the cursed journey.

Kintana looked around the tavern. There were monkeys of every size and colour. They chattered and preened their masters and each other. The beams were filled with brightly plumed parrots, hornbills and other exotic birds that squawked and sang and flapped their wings. There were bird droppings over all the furniture and one big dollop had even splattered into one of the pirate's drinks! *There are more animals here than in our pet shop!* thought Kintana.

The bar was a lovely dark wood that stretched the length of the room. From one end to the other it was covered with full and empty rum glasses, all filthy.

Kintana searched for Pa, ignoring the squelching noises as she crossed the sticky floor. The spilt beer was bad enough, but there was an equal measure of monkey poo.

"*Mbola tsara*! Hello!" said the barman, wiping out a glass with a dirty cloth. "I thought you'd gone to sea!"

"It was a round trip."

"Your Pa will be pleased. He's in the corner with your mates from *The Nine Sails*."

Kintana made her way past tables packed with more pirates and animals. She was just stepping round giant snails, skinks, boas, radiated tortoises and mongooses when she heard Pa's familiar voice!

"*A sailor went to shea, shea, shea*
"*He was as happy as could be, be, be,*"
"*Till he needed a w*—Kinshana!"

Pa was sat at an oval, wooden table with Gangrene, Pots and Captain Tortuga.

Kintana took a deep breath and sat down on the bench next to him.

"You've come back to shee your old Pa, at last. Aw, that'sh lovely. Did you like being a pirate?"

"*Pa?*" Captain Tortuga cocked his head to one side. "You're Israel Hands's daughter?"

Gangrene choked on his drink, his face turning purple. "Bloomin' 'eck!"

"You hired Tremblin' Hands's little girl as a cabin boy!" laughed Pots.

"I told you shnot to call me that." Pa slammed his empty glass down on the table. "I shtill remember 'ow to use my cutlassh," he slurred, "and I'd happily tesht its sharpness on you."

"Now, now, Israel. I'm sure your blade's not as sharp as your tongue," soothed Gangrene, stroking his wiry, grey plait.

I've got to persuade Pa to come home before he says something he regrets, thought Kintana. "Are you hungry, Pa? I was going to make a nice stew for your tea."

"Aww, ishn't she wondershful. I'm so proud of you Kinshana, I sham. Let me getsh you a drink, love. What will you have? A glassh of palm wine or a rum punch maybe?"

"Don't be silly, Pa, you know I don't drink."

"Oh, that'sh right. Well, I'll have one."

Gangrene stood up. "I'll get another round in."

"Busy in here tonight," said Tortuga.

Kintana looked around; it was true. Every member of *The Nine Sails* crew was in the tavern, dressed in their best coloured silks. She could see Croak, Spike and Zachariah sitting together at another nearby table. They had bowls of what looked like bar snacks in front of them, but then she realised they were worms, cockroaches and flies for their pets.

Captain Tortuga massaged his bald head, "The barkeeper tells me this place has been deserted, except for your Pa."

Kintana chewed on her bottom lip.

"Thish island used to be a real pirate's kingdom, but thingsh change," said Pa. "People leave."

"What a good idea," said Tortuga. "You must be wanting to get home to catch up with your daughter."

"Did I shtell you that I shtarted out as a cabin boy, jusht like you Kintana." He squeezed her tight. "A great little powder monkey I was, runnin' acrossh the crowded wet deck, tryin' not to shlip carryin' ladles of gunpowder."

Kintana jumped as Gangrene returned, slapping a tray of drinks on to the table. He passed a monogrammed metal tankard to Captain Tortuga. Then slid on to the bench next to him.

Kintana pushed some nuts towards Pa, hoping it would help sober him up.

"You're a good man, Gangrene. I know you will always support me." Tortuga sipped at his new drink. "Ooh, what is this? It's got a bit of a kick. Nice flavour too."

Gangrene smiled. "I'm glad you like it, Captain. It's a special brew just for you."

"Go easy though, it's strong stuff – it might have you doing all sorts before you know it!" Pots laughed.

Kintana stuffed a handful of nuts into her mouth. They were up to something.

Captain Tortuga took a big swig. "It's really refreshing, goes down like syrup. Too many of these and I'll be cartwheeling back to *The Nine Sails* without a care."

"I'll get you another, Captain, my treat." The quartermaster was up again.

"Yes, another drink," he said in a strange hypnotic voice. "Whatever you say, Mr Gangrene."

Kintana frowned. The drink must be really strong – the captain's eyes were already glazed.

A moment later, Gangrene had returned with a refill. "Drink up, Captain."

"Drink up," repeated Tortuga, gulping down the second tankard full.

Gangrene took Snuffles out of his shirt, sat him on the table and fed him titbits from his pocket. He leaned in and whispered to his pet, "Looks like one was enough, but two will make sure."

"Two will make sure," repeated the captain, wiping his mouth clean.

Gangrene grinned. "It's good to have a drink together."

"Yes, it's good to have a drink together," repeated Captain Tortuga.

Kintana pretended to be struggling to get her pa up from the table, so she could keep listening.

"We're good friends aren't we, Captain?"

"Good friends."

He's repeating everything Gangrene says, thought Kintana.

"And friends help each other."

"Help each other," he repeated.

Gangrene stood up. "Let's go outside and I'll explain . . ."

"Yes, let's go outside . . ." replied Tortuga, getting up . . . "and you'll explain."

"Excellent." Gangrene put an arm round him, and Pots jumped up to assist from the other side.

"Fresh air sounds just the tonic," said Kintana. She hooked Pa under his arm and pulled him up. He staggered a bit, but somehow, she managed to get him through the tavern, and finally outside.

Gangrene and Pots were hurrying away with the captain. *What are they planning next?* she wondered, struggling to keep Pa upright.

The sun beat down, and Kintana felt sticky with sweat. Pa's wooden leg kept sinking into the dirt and she moaned with frustration at being unable to keep up with the other pirates. She'd have to give up, for now.

Kintana sniffed back a tear. She thought it would be a relief to be home, but she felt worse than ever.

Chapter Fifteen

THE PIRATE CEMETERY

NEXT MORNING, KINTANA MADE SOME PORRIDGE and filled her flask with water, then tried to persuade Pa to join her at the trial. But he refused to get out of bed, saying he was too tired, too sick. "You shouldn't have drunk so much," she scolded.

She left him to sleep, grabbed her pirate hat, and set off for the old fort, alone.

Kintana walked briskly from the pet shop to the edge of Pirate Island where she could cross the channel to Nosy Boraha.

A line of carved out wooden pirogues were secured at the water's edge. She dragged one of the hand-carved boats out, pushed it into the sea and clambered inside. Then Kintana scooped up the oar and began to paddle her way across the channel to the other side.

Once she'd reached the opposite shore, Kintana abandoned the pirogue and trudged to the crossroads. She paused at the traveller's palm tree, then took the path to the left that stretched on northwards to the old fort. After a fifteen-minute walk it finally loomed ahead of her, its tall wooden ramparts casting a gloomy shadow.

She passed through the gatehouse and into the open courtyard which was being used as a makeshift courtroom. Rows of crude wooden benches had been set out for spectators. There was a large chair for the judge, a dock for the accused to stand in and a lectern for the witnesses to stand at – but the place was in total chaos!

Croak was standing on one of the benches screaming, "Order! Order!" as furniture was lobbed across the yard.

Pirates were wrestling on the floor. Others were pushing and shoving each other.

Bartholomew was being shielded by Spike and Zachariah. The boy was weeping. He had a huge black eye.

Kintana felt awful. *Poor Bartholomew!* "What happened?" she called.

"Captain Tortuga didn't show up!" Zachariah shouted back, blocking flying punches and kicks. "'e was supposed to 'ear the evidence . . ."

"The main witnesses haven't shown up either!" shouted Spike, mopping blood from his cut lip. "It turned into a brawl!"

Kintana hollered to them. "But I've come to give evidence! Bartholomew is innocent."

Zachariah shrugged. "We've had to postpone, and that didn't go down well with the rest of the crew. We've got to get the lad safely back to his cell before he's killed!"

Bartholomew began to wail as they dragged him out of the makeshift courtroom.

Kintana ducked as someone threw a chair and made a dash for the outside.

It didn't make sense. Why would Gangrene set up Bartholomew to take the blame for the missing flag, then not turn up to see him convicted?

She stumbled away from the old fort. She had been awake all night, planning what to say, never thinking for one moment that there would be no trial to speak at!

"Kintana! Kintana!" squawked Polly, swooping into view. "You've got to come! Quick!"

"What's wrong now?" she asked, with a sinking feeling.

"I've just seen Gangrene and Pots – they had a hessian sack and spades – I think they're going after the treasure!"

"Did they say where they were going?"

"Don't worry I can catch up with them!" Polly shot off again.

She rushed after the parrot, following the pathway to the crossroads.

When Kintana finally reached it there was no sign of Polly. She looked around in confusion, wondering which way the pirates had gone. There were three options: south – towards the pirate cemetery, inland to the east, or west back to the pirogues and home.

"What are you looking for?" asked a higher-pitched squawky voice.

Kintana looked up at the traveller's palm tree. It was another vasa parrot! Only this one must be a female, she realised, noting her yellow head. The parrot must be ready for breeding if she'd lost all her grey plumes.

Polly gave a whistle of delight. "Esther!" He flew up to perch beside her. "I've been looking for you everywhere, my darling."

"Don't call me darling, not when you've been gone weeks!" She turned her back on him.

"Esther, my sweetness, you know you are the only parrot for me. I didn't leave you – I was captured!"

"Captured?" She hopped round, to face him again. "Oh! My poor true love. What happened."

"I was trapped on a pirate ship!"

"Oh, Polly!" She nuzzled him with her beak.

He whistled with delight.

"I didn't know you had a girlfriend!" whispered Kintana.

"A good-looking bird like me! Of course I have!" Polly gave another little whistle.

"Pleased to meet you, Esther," said Kintana.

"Likewise," she swung upside down and fanned out her tail feathers.

"Isn't she the most beautiful parrot, you've ever seen," said Polly.

"Definitely," she replied.

Esther lowered her head, shyly.

"Kintana and I are spying on Gangrene and Pots, two pirates from *The Nine Sails*, the ship I was captured on."

"Did you see which way they went?"

"Oh yes," said Esther. "They took that path, towards the cemetery."

Kintana knew the cemetery well. It was the burial place for everyone on Pirate Island, not just buccaneers. Her own mama was buried there, and she and Pa would go from time to time to lay fresh flowers at her grave. She wrinkled her nose. Why were Gangrene and Pots going there?

"Follow me." Kintana continued along the beaten path, her legs splashed with brown sludge and scratched by spiky weeds. She pushed on through the long grass and shrubs until she reached the top of the hill.

The cemetery looked out over the sea and Pirate Island. There was an air of tranquillity about the place. The grass had been scorched by the sun and the coconut palms round the edge cast leafy shadows on to the hallowed ground.

Kintana tucked herself in behind a thick palm tree at the entrance to the graveyard and beckoned the parrots nearer.

They landed at her feet. Esther cocked her head to one side, "Hmm, which one is Gangrene?"

"The one with the big rat!" said Polly.

"I'm going to fly over there and peck his eyes out."

"Esther!" Polly shook his head. But Kintana could tell he was pleased.

The female parrot flapped her wings. "They're up to something bad. Pirates are always up to something bad."

The pirates's graves were all together at the far end of the cemetery in the shadow of several large palm trees. Gangrene was studying the headstones. Some bore inscriptions, one clearly had the skull and crossbones on it, and another was topped with a cross.

"We need to get closer," said Kintana.

"I'll go," said Polly. "It's too risky for you; Gangrene might see you."

Kintana shrugged. "I don't care, I'm not scared of him." *That's not true*, she thought, *but if I talk confidently, it might make me feel braver*. She sneaked around the perimeter of the cemetery, dodging between palm trees until she had found a good spot behind a particularly thick trunk. Polly and Esther flew low down and settled on the ground beside her.

Gangrene crouched and opened a hessian sack. He pulled out something round and hairy. The stench of vinegar filled the air.

Kintana covered her mouth, almost retching.

"Erghhh!" cried Gangrene. "It stinks worse than your feet."

Kintana took out Pa's spyglass to see what it was, bringing the viewfinder to her eye. She panned, then yanked the spyglass away.

It was a head! A human head! Her stomach lurched again. It was all bloated and greyish green. Kintana wrapped her arms around her middle to calm herself. She wanted to run for home.

No. She had to see what they were up to. For Bartholomew's sake, if nothing else. She breathed deeply. She had to know what Gangrene and Pots were going to do next.

Kintana made herself look again. She lifted Pa's spyglass.

The head had plaited hair, tied with strips of faded ribbon, and a long. dark, tangled beard, like sea snakes.

She knew whose it was.

Blackbeard's!

Chapter Sixteen

GRAVE TROUBLE

KINTANA RECOILED – SOMEHOW GANGRENE AND Pots had got hold of Captain Blackbeard's decapitated head. The slow-burning fuses in his hair and beard, that he had loved lighting during attacks, were sodden. No longer would they plume out thick, black smoke.

Gangrene grasped Blackbeard's hair; it looked greasy and slippery. The captain's face was all soggy and bloated – Blackbeard looked as horrible as he smelled.

"Here." The quartermaster passed the head to the cook, wiping his gloopy hands on his apron. Then Pots carried the head over to a coconut palm and placed it reverently on the ground.

"Pass us your knife. I'm thirsty," said Gangrene, taking off a large leather satchel before removing his blue jacket. He picked up a coconut from the ground.

Pots handed the blade over and the quartermaster gave the

coconut a crack and drank the watery milk. He gave his mouth a wipe. "Don't worry, I'll look after your knife."

The cook looked alarmed. "But it's mine!"

"You might accidentally cut yourself." Gangrene pushed the knife into his belt.

"But you've already got the cat o'nine tails."

Gangrene patted his waistcoat. "And don't you forget it."

Pots grunted and picked up a spade.

Gangrene pointed to an unmarked grave next to a large, spiky cactus. The mound of soil on top looked the freshest. "That's where we buried Eyeball. Get diggin'."

They must be planning to bury Blackbeard's head next to the navigator, Kintana decided.

Gangrene reached into his semi-open shirt and gently lifted out his giant jumping rat. "Were you all snug as a bug?" he asked, kissing his pet's nose. He placed Snuffles on the ground. "Stay there for Daddy. I'll find you a nice worm, if you're good." He grabbed the other spade and joined Pots. "These shovels will be handy for fendin' off any mad monkeys too," he joked.

Snuffles began digging with his claws.

"Look at him copyin' me," Gangrene laughed, as he rested against his spade for a moment.

Pots scowled. "I don't know why you carry him round like a baby, you should have left him on the ship."

Gangrene chucked his shovel of soil at Pots. "He's too little to be left on his own."

The cook wiped himself clean and continued digging. He looked longingly at Gangrene's flask, but the pirate never offered it to him.

"When I die, I want to be buried at sea," said Pots, "not stuck in a box in the ground. No sew me up in my old hammock and let the briny have me."

The pirates were now a couple of feet down. Above them, they had formed an ever-growing pile of sandy soil.

They increased their efforts.

Snuffles was digging faster and harder too. Kintana could barely see him as he burrowed deeper.

There was a sound of metal hitting wood. "I think we've reached the coffin," called Pots.

Now what are they going to do? Kintana worried.

Gangrene wiped his brow. "Excellent."

The giant jumping rat was still digging a tunnel at the side of the coffin.

"Snuffles, come out of there!" Gangrene wailed.

But it was too late his pet had disappeared into it. "Don't worry," said Pots. "Your rat will come out again when he gets hungry."

Gangrene growled, picked up his spade and flipped it over so it became a weapon.

Pots staggered back.

Kintana clasped a hand over her mouth. He was going to hit him with it!

Then he jerked round. "Tortuga!" Gangrene dropped the spade and scrambled out of the hole.

The captain was entering the cemetery, but there was something strange about him. He spoke not a word his face was expressionless; his eyes glazed over. *He's still under the effects of that drink they gave him*, Kintana realised, *but how can that be?*

"Where have you been?" spat Gangrene.

"Where have I been?" repeated Tortuga, rubbing between his eyes.

He's still speaking in that strange monotone voice, it's as though in a hypnotic trance, thought Kintana.

"Perhaps my potion was too strong," said Pots.

Gangrene grunted. "Well, you're here now."

"Here now," repeated Tortuga.

"He's worse than a parrot," muttered Pots.

Gangrene snorted. "We need to clear around the coffin." He thrust his spade at Tortuga. "Dig."

"Dig," repeated Captain Tortuga. He climbed down into the hole and started scooping up the remaining soil around the coffin.

Tortuga began to sing in rhythm with his rapid digging –

> *"Don't go down to the galley,*
> *Unless you want a shock,*
> *'Cause there's rats in the hold,*
> *And your head's on the block . . .*

Gangrene kept watch as Tortuga and Pots dug, beads of sweat on their foreheads as they toiled.

> *"The cook boils up trouble,*
> *He makes a special stock,*
> *There's spices and herbs,*
> *And a trace of hemlock . . ."*

"Quiet!" ordered Gangrene.

Tortuga clammed up immediately.

Kintana couldn't understand why the captain was being so submissive. *It must be the potion.*

Gangrene lowered himself into the hole.

They had fully exposed the coffin. It looked almost new.

"We've got to get the body out." Gangrene stood at the head end. "Pots, you take the bottom. Tortuga, you take the weight in the middle."

The pirates slowly lifted the coffin and shifted it on to the bank next to the hole.

Gangrene used the edge of his spade to prise the lid. "You can take the body out," he ordered.

Kintana wanted to shake them all; make the pirates stop this desecration.

Pots shook his head. "I don't want to touch him, poor Eyeball."

"You've got to." said Gangrene. "If you want to bring Captain Blackbeard back to life!"

Kintana couldn't believe her ears. *How on earth do they think they can do that?*

"Prop the body against that headstone . . ." said Gangrene. Kintana turned her face away, knowing Pots and Tortuga were now lifting Eyeball's body out of the coffin. "I'll get the book . . ."

Book? It must be the one Gangrene had stolen from the captain's drawer.

"He's taking it out of his satchel," said Esther.

Kintana made herself look. She was relieved to see Pots and Tortuga had covered the body with a large piece of hessian. She recognised the gold letters on the book's cover even from a distance – *Curses and Charms.*

Gangrene reached into his pocket. "Of course, we need this

too . . ." He pulled out a small skeletal hand with a long bony, middle finger.

"Oh no!" Kintana covered her eyes. "He's brought the aye-aye hand I gave him!"

"I've got a bad feeling," said Polly, shielding Esther's eyes with his wing.

Me too, Kintana thought.

"A hand?" questioned the cook, dismissively.

"Not just any hand," said Gangrene, "This, my friend, is an aye-aye paw – and it is deadly!"

Kintana shuddered. *It's not true*, she told herself. Some people said if an aye-aye pointed their long middle finger at you, then you would drop down dead. But she'd never heard of an aye-aye doing anyone any harm. Pa said the aye-aye might look strange, with its big ears and teeth, but it was a shy, nocturnal animal that was only interested in tapping out insect larvae from trees with that extra-long digit.

"Don't worry, I'm not going to kill you," teased Gangrene, snapping the middle finger from the rest of the hand. "Actually, thanks to this spell we can use the aye-aye's power to raise the dead!"

The quartermaster took Tortuga's hand and turned it palm up, placing the thin, bony finger on it. "It takes a captain to wake a captain."

Kintana gasped. So that's why they needed Captain Tortuga's assistance!

"You need me too," Pots asserted.

"Of course I do." Gangrene rolled up his sleeves. "I need you to fetch Blackbeard's head."

Pots sighed and walked over to the base of the coconut tree and lifted up the pickled head.

"Time to swap the heads over." Gangrene drew his cutlass.

Kintana could watch no more.

Chapter Seventeen

WAKING THE DEAD

A MINUTE LATER ESTHER NUDGED KINTANA GENTLY with her beak. "It's ... done."

"I should have stopped them ..." she wiped tears from her face.

"There was nothing you could do," said Polly.

Pots had placed Blackbeard's sloppy head on top of Eyeball's newly severed neck. There were thick stitches holding the two parts together. Pirates had to be skilled with a needle, but this was not how their sail-mending skills should be used. Kintana swallowed hard and forced herself to keep watching.

"Tie in some fresh flares," Gangrene ordered.

Pots rubbed round his eyepatch, then pulled some flares out of his pocket. He switched the damp ones in Blackbeard's black hair with dry ones.

Gangrene flicked through the pages of the *Curses and Charms* book, until he found what he was looking for. "Here it is . . . Captain, hold the aye-aye finger high above your head."

Tortuga lifted the bone.

"Now turn the finger three times – clockwise."

Tortuga turned it round and round and round to the right.

The temperature plummeted. Black rain clouds far out at sea began to move in as though lured in by the finger.

"I'm scared," Kintana whispered.

"Us too," said Polly, shaking his feathers. Esther tucked herself into his side.

A shadow fell over the corpse and Blackbeard's head and then there was a sudden flash of light.

The flares tied in the captain's hair ignited. They fizzed and glowed yellow-red, billowing thick, black smoke.

"It's working!" cried Pots.

Kintana clasped her hand to her mouth.

"Your role is over," Gangrene addressed Tortuga and took the aye-aye finger from him. "You can return to *The Nine Sails* now, Captain."

"Return," said Tortuga. He started to walk away, unblinking.

Gangrene waited for the captain to exit the graveyard. "My turn!" He raised the aye-aye finger above his head. "Three more turns and I will have control."

Pots counted – "one, two, three."

"*Revivo!*" shouted Gangrene.

There was a bright flash of lightening. Kintana shielded her eyes.

A loud crash of thunder ricocheted across the graveyard, followed by a rumbling.

The sky darkened and a cold chill filled the air. Kintana's skin was goosebumped all over.

The body started to twitch – its fingers flexing first, then its toes. Kintana gasped.

"It's working," cried Pots.

Gangrene slammed the book shut and pushed it back into his satchel, then threw it on the ground. "I told you it would."

The body stretched out its legs, the knees seemed stiff and jerky at first. Then it pushed its hands into the dirt to give itself more force as it drew itself up to full height, looming over Gangrene and Pots.

The head was slowest to awake. The neck began to twist first, as though the circulation wasn't used to flowing between the fused body parts.

Blackbeard's squelchy grey face began to spasm, the muscles in his cheeks pulsed, his lips trembled. Finally, his eyes flashed open – the milky pupils focusing on the pirates.

Kintana trembled as Blackbeard's swollen lips parted, and a gut-wrenching roar echoed out.

Blackbeard thrust his arm out, making a stabbing motion, then he lowered his head, taking in his empty hand.

"Where's my sword?" he growled. He rotated his hand; the bone was starting to show through in places.

Blackbeard made a fist and shook it. "What have you done!"

"You're alive!" Gangrene tossed the aye-aye finger over his shoulder and rushed forward.

"This might be my only chance," Kintana whispered to the parrots. "I need to get that book and find a way to undo the spell."

Blackbeard roared. "Where's my ship? And what's that stink?" He sniffed the air loudly. "Why do I whiff of vinegar?"

"It's your head," said Pots. "I preserved it."

"Wait! I know you. You're the cook." The captain turned and pointed his finger at Gangrene. "But you, I don't know."

"I'm quartermaster on *The Nine Sails*. Mister Gangrene . . ." he held out his hand, then retracted it, hastily.

"*The Nine Sails*? Never heard of it." Blackbeard slumped against the headstone. He put a hand to his head, as though dizzy. "Where's my ship?"

"It was captured," said Pots. "You were badly hurt, in a battle. Don't you remember, Captain?"

Kintana got on to her hands and knees and crawled through the foliage. The satchel lay at Gangrene's feet. How was she going to get it?

Blackbeard's eyes sparked. "I would not surrender – but . . . but . . ." He rubbed his forehead as if trying to recall what had happened next. Loose bits of skin flaked off. He gasped. "I was *shot* . . ."

"Five times," said Pots, reverently.

"and stabbed!"

"Twenty times . . ." Pots concurred.

Blackbeard touched his neck. "I was dying – and then . . ." he patted a hand all over his torso, searching for wounds. "Something's wrong." He staggered back. "This is not my body!" He moaned. "What nightmare is this? Am I in hell?"

"You're in a pirate's paradise, Captain," said Pots.

Blackbeard furrowed his brow. "Paradise? This looks like a graveyard!"

Gangrene picked up the satchel and swung it over his shoulder. "It is."

"Oh no!" said Polly. "You'll never get the book now!"

Chapter Eighteen

BREAKING THE SPELL

KINTANA TOOK A DEEP BREATH, WILLING COURAGE. "I have to find that aye-aye finger, maybe I can use it to break the spell."

"Go now," said Esther. "I'll whistle if I think they're looking your way."

Kintana got on her hands and knees and began to crawl further round the edge of the cemetery. Polly hopped alongside her.

Blackbeard was laughing, but there was no warmth in the sound. "You'd better explain exactly what is going on . . ."

"The crew were dragged away by your enemy, Maynard, for interrogation," Pots continued. "I'd avoided capture, so I was able to sneak back on to deck to salvage your head."

"It was too late for your body," said Gangrene, matter-of-factly. "They'd chucked it overboard for the sharks to eat."

Kintana kept listening as she neared the spot where the aye-aye finger had been flung.

Pots closed his eyes. "They hung your head from the ship's bow. I couldn't leave you like that. Desecrated! I stole it and swore to protect your remains ever since."

I have to be brave, Kintana told herself. She took a deep breath and pushed her hands into the bush.

"We got you a new body and reanimated you," finished Gangrene.

Blackbeard roared. "You dug up a corpse and stuck my head on top! Please, tell me what possessed you!"

"Treasure!" said Gangrene. "You should be able to understand that. We need your half of the riddle."

Kintana paused. "Another riddle!" she whispered to Polly.

Blackbeard narrowed his eyes. "What riddle? I know nothing about any riddle."

"Don't you remember?" asked Pots. "I told you that Captain Kidd had buried his treasure on Nosy Boraha."

"Did you?" Blackbeard looked confused.

Pots grimaced. "Kidd wrote a riddle so he could find his way back to it, something about east and west, but I can't remember the rest.

"Only Kidd never got the chance to return what with him being dead," Pots continued. "Before his execution, Kidd entrusted me with the riddle – only it was useless to me without a ship to take me back to Madagascar.

"I asked captain after captain to take me on as cook, only my culinary reputation went against me. You were my last chance, Captain. I knew I had no choice but to confide in you. You must remember? I told you all about Kidd's treasure and the riddle.

I tore the paper in two and we each kept half, as a bond. Only then you died, and I couldn't find where you had hidden your piece."

"Luckily, this sad tale has a surprise happy endin'," said Gangrene. "This time, I was persuaded to hire Pots, on the understandin' that we would split Kidd's gold and jewels between us! We brought your head back to Nosy Boraha, and with a little dark magic – well here you are!"

"So, if you could tell us where your part of the riddle is . . ." said Pots.

Blackbeard slammed his fist down on the headstone and his thumb dropped off. "I never could stand you, Pots. Worse cook I've ever known, nearly poisoned me three times. I never trust other pirates, you good for nothing seadogs! *You* should give ME your half of the riddle."

"That's not fair!" cried Pots. "I was always loyal, not like that traitor Israel Hands . . ."

Kintana's ears pricked up at the mention of her pa.

"Israel was the one—"

"I've never handed over anything of mine willingly in my life!" said Blackbeard. "Did you really think I would give up my half of the riddle and stroll off into the sunset! Think again Fish Face!"

"There's going to be blood spilled," said Polly.

Kintana shushed him and continued to search.

Pots had lowered his head. "We didn't mean to offend," he stuttered.

Kintana patted around. She pulled out a twig. Then searched some more.

"We could negotiate," said Gangrene smarmily. "Come to a deal, an agreement."

"How about we agree that I kill the pair of you! You're nothing but dirty, common thieves!" Blackbeard lurched forward, screaming curses and threats.

Gangrene drew his cutlass and slashed it defensively.

Blackbeard's laughter boomed. "You can't kill me. I'm invincible!"

Just in time, Kintana's hand touched something bone-like. She swallowed down her fear, then grasped the aye-aye finger and pulled it out.

"Well done," said Polly. "Now what?"

"I don't know," replied Kintana, her voice quavering.

"You *have* to reverse the spell," said Esther.

"That's it," said Kintana, excitedly. "Gangrene said the aye-aye finger had to be turned clockwise."

"What's clockwise?" asked Polly.

"No idea, but he turned it in this direction," she wiggled her own finger round to the right. "What if I did it in reverse – backwards!"

"Try it!" said Esther.

Kintana lifted the aye-aye finger high above her head then turned it three times anti-clockwise, desperately hoping it would undo the spell.

The rain clouds suddenly blew in overhead, plunging the cemetery into darkness. A fierce wind picked up, sending leaves and twigs hurtling across the ground. Kintana wrapped an arm round a thin palm tree to stop herself from being swept away, the aye-aye finger clutched in her hand. With her other hand, she held pa's hat tightly against her head.

Blackbeard was being held back by the wind. He howled with frustration.

Pots was on his knees, whimpering.

Gangrene shielded his eyes against the dust. "What was on the other half of the paper?" he bellowed. His voice lost against the roaring gale. "Give me the rest of the riddle!"

"NEVER!"

Strong gusts whipped across the graves. The soil was crumbling, as though something was just under the surface, something trying to get out.

Gangrene saw it too. "It's Snuffles," he cried, battling through the wind and throwing himself down on to the ground. "Daddy's here. I'll keep you safe, baby."

But it wasn't the giant jumping rat pushing up through the surface. It was a skeletal hand!

Kintana screamed; the spell must have woken another pirate! That wasn't the plan!

The skeleton was pushing up through the grave like an evil plant, the hand feeling around like a confused spider.

"Batten down the hatches!" roared Blackbeard. "All hands on deck!"

Gangrene and Pots staggered back.

The other mounds were splitting open as more bony fingers poked through the surface and began to dig their way out.

"What have I done?" Kintana wailed, desperately turning the aye-aye finger this way and that. "I've woken up all the dead pirates!"

The skeletons were getting to their feet. There were seven of them, they staggered forward.

"That's it, men!" whooped Blackbeard. "Attack! Attack!"

The pirate skeletons were gathering, circling slowly round Gangrene and Pots.

Blackbeard battled against the storm, head down, moving in for the kill.

Gangrene fumbled for the cat o'nine tails.

"Sssttttooppp!" squealed Pots, as a skeleton suddenly leapt forward, whipped him upside down, and shook him violently. A torn piece of paper escaped from behind his eyepatch and was blown into the air. "The riddle!"

Blackbeard pushed Gangrene on to his back, knocking the cat o'nine tails from his hand. Then the captain grabbed him by the ankles and dragged him towards the open grave. The quartermaster kicked out, crying for help.

A strong gust sent the paper swirling higher and higher.

"Polly! Esther! Get that riddle!" pleaded Kintana.

The parrots soared into the air, chasing the paper, but each time they closed in on it, it spiralled out of reach.

"Hurry!" Kintana risked a glance at the pirates. Pots was being pulled from side to side by two skeletons, like he was in the middle of a tug of war. While Gangrene was being yanked ever closer to the coffin.

The parrots were gaining height, despite the wind. They were right on top of the paper. Esther opened her beak and snapped down hard.

Kintana breathed a sigh of relief on seeing the riddle safely clamped in her beak.

The parrots swooped down, and Esther presented the paper with a bow of her head.

"Who's a clever girl," said Polly, proudly.

"We don't want the riddle blowing away again," said Kintana. She tucked the aye-aye finger under her armpit and took off her hat. She pulled out one of the pins holding back the brim and used it to secure the paper to the felt. "That should do it."

She wiped the grit from her eyes. *Now for the spell. There must be a way to break it*, she thought. *But how to break the spell?* She studied the aye-aye finger. *It looks so thin and fragile. So easy to break – Oh! Maybe that's the answer!* Kintana grasped the bone with her fingers and thumbs. Then she flicked her wrists hard.

SNAP!

In the same instant there was a deafening crack of thunder. The rainclouds burst dowsing the cemetery.

Blackbeard slithered to the ground, as the life drained from him.

The other pirates were crumbling or sliding back down into their own graves.

The cook wept as the two skeletons collapsed at his feet.

Gangrene flailed his arms and legs, trying to get out of the coffin.

Kintana shoved the broken aye-aye finger into her jacket pocket.

"You did it!" squawked Polly, "but don't stand round gloating."

"Those two are going to want their riddle back," agreed Esther.

Gangrene was clambering out of the grave and calling for Pots to get up.

Kintana tugged her hat down tight on her head and ran.

Chapter Nineteen

THE RIDDLE

KINTANA SPRINTED ALL THE WAY DOWN THE path, until she was back at the crossing to Pirate Island. She was relieved to find the pirogue was still where she had hidden it but, as she got closer, she realised there was already someone sitting in it.

"Hello, Captain," she said soothingly.

Tortuga blinked his eyes several times. "What happened? Where am I?"

"You're on Nosy Boraha, Captain, but I'm going to take you back to *The Nine Sails.*"

"I feel like I have woken from the strangest dream," he said. "The air was rancid and there was this head . . ." he grimaced.

Kintana placed a hand on his shoulder, "It's all right. You're safe now."

Tortuga jolted his head round, as though seeing her for the

first time. He clutched her jacket lapels. "Gangrene and Pots were there! They made me—" he released her and held his head in his hands . . . "They made me dig up a body."

"What they did was awful," said Kintana. "Unspeakable, but it's not your fault, Captain, you were in a trance, they drugged you."

Tortuga lifted his head. "Drugged?"

"Yes, they laced your drink with something. It made you do whatever they said."

"But that's impossible . . . unless . . ." – he massaged his temple – "they had the *Curses and Charms* book," his eyes were wide now, "and an aye-aye finger!"

"They don't have the finger any more, but they still have your book."

Tortuga cupped his hands around her face "Kintana, they stole my book," he was staring at her hard. "They are thieves. I'm beginning to think you were right. Bartholomew didn't steal the flag – what if it was Gangrene and Pots?"

"You're right, Captain. Bartholomew is innocent. You must release him! But first I want you to see the dokotera. I'm taking you back to *The Nine Sails*."

☠

"Kintana!" Pa ran towards her as she made her way to the harbour with Captain Tortuga. "I've been so worried about you. Where have you been? I've been lookin' all over Pirate Island for you!"

He wrapped his arms round her and squeezed her. It felt good to be in his arms, warm and protected.

"It's a long story," Kintana replied once he'd released her. "I need to find Spike, the ship's dokotera." She guided Tortuga towards the gangplank. "Let's get you to your cabin, Captain."

"I'm sorry I got in such a state yesterday," said Pa, as they stepped on to the ramp. "You know I'm not a big drinker, but I was feelin' sorry for myself and when the crew came in, I joined in with the boozing. Pirates are always generous when they first come home – Gangrene must have bought me at least three mugs of rum."

"He wasn't being generous, Pa, he was handing out the drinks so he could slip the captain a potion."

"A potion?" asked Pa, pausing on deck. "What kind of potion?"

"One that gave him complete control over my mind," said Tortuga. "It was awful!"

"The good news is the captain is going to drop the charges against my friend, Bartholomew, and release him," added Kintana. "I'll explain properly, later . . ."

She found Spike, the dokotera, along with Croak and Zachariah playing a game of dice on deck. She beckoned them into the captain's quarters and explained that Tortuga had been given a drug.

The dokotera asked the captain to follow his finger with his eyes then asked him some basic questions to test his memory and consciousness.

"He seems fine," said Spike, satisfied.

Tortuga picked up a quill pen and began to write on a piece of parchment. "I want you to take my orders to the old fort. They are to release Bartholomew at once."

"Yes, Captain," replied Croak.

"I'll keep watch for any sign of Gangrene and Pots," said Zachariah. "Though I doubt they'll be so foolish as to come back to Pirate Island tonight."

"You should get some rest, Captain, in case of relapse," added Spike. "I recommend at least a day's recuperation to make sure whatever drug you have been given has left your system. You can't risk a relapse. No treasure hunting for you!"

"Thank you dokotera. Believe me, I have other priorities. Once I am rested, I need to inspect my collection. They had my aye-aye hand. I fear they may have stolen more. I must check my inventory."

"And I will investigate the ship's galley," said Spike. "I want to know what was in that drink."

"I'll come with you," said Kintana. "I might be able to help."

"Not until you've had something to eat," said Pa. "I'll prepare somethin' for us."

"A good meal would benefit the captain too," agreed Spike. "Let's go."

They made their way down to the galley.

It was cold and dark inside. Kintana lit a candle and Pa started to make a fire.

Whiskers was curled up under the table – she was lying on her side looking lethargic.

"Poor thing has been left without food or water. I'll get her a drink first," said Kintana.

Pa started gathering some vegetables. "I'll make a quick lasopy." He picked up a knife and started peeling.

Kintana's stomach rumbled at the thought of the traditional Malagasy soup.

Spike searched for evidence of the potion. "Ah ha," he said, pointing to the bunches of dried herbs suspended from the ceiling. "These are used in sleeping draughts . . ."

"I think Pots might have put some in the special stew," said

Kintana, "the one meant for the captain, that Gangrene ate by mistake."

Spike was angry. "Any of these have side effects which could make a patient confused or vulnerable to suggestion. I'll tell Tortuga to have them all destroyed."

Kintana needed something to lower into the barrel for the water. She picked up a large empty jar; there was a slight odour of pickled onions, but it would have to do.

The fossa began to hiss loudly.

"What's wrong girl? I'm just getting you some water," she looked closer at the jar. Three black hairs were stuck to the side of the glass. Kintana swallowed. *I think I know where they were storing Blackbeard's head. Of course, the captain was the 'him' they were talking about protecting!*

She wiped her fingers furiously against her clothes. Then found a bowl, instead, and filled it with water. She put it on the floor, and the fossa took a long drink.

Pa put the lasopy on the fire. "I'll bring it through when it's done," he said. "Why don't you take Whiskers on deck for some fresh air. She can't enjoy being cooped up in here all the time."

Kintana smiled. "All right, Pa. Come on, Whiskers."

But as soon as Kintana opened the galley door, the fossa sprang past her – jinking across the deck and over the gangway.

"That was some break for freedom," said Spike.

"She's probably gone looking for Pots," said Kintana.

"In that mood, he'd better hope she doesn't find him!" he replied.

☠

"You look a little better, Captain," said Spike as they sat down to eat, an hour later.

"I feel better, Dokotera," answered Tortuga. "And I am sure this soup will do me the world of good!"

Pa placed the pan in the centre of the table and dished it into bowls.

Tortuga sipped from a spoon. "Delicious!"

The others tucked in.

The lasopy was steaming hot so Kintana took off her pirate hat to wipe her brow.

She undid the pins holding up the brim. But was surprised to find there was not one piece of paper – but two!

"Oh!" she said, picking them up, and frowning as she studied them. "I don't understand."

"What are they?" asked Pa.

"It's a riddle . . ." Kintana studied them closely – the two pieces of paper had been torn down one side and they fitted together perfectly. "But I have both parts – when I should only have *one*. Pots only had one piece, I heard him tell Blackbeard that was why they needed to resurrect him – so they could get the second. That was the piece I fastened inside my hat - so how did this other piece get here?"

"Where did you get the hat?" asked Tortuga, his eyebrow raised.

"It's Pa's. He gave it to me."

Pa got up hastily and started gathering the bowls.

"*Pa?*"

He sighed. "That's not exactly true . . . I mean it became mine."

"What do you mean, *became* yours?" asked Kintana.

Pa put the bowls down again. "It was Blackbeard's. I kept it after he was killed, as a kind of memento."

Kintana sat back in her chair, "Blackbeard's!"

"Look, you can still see some of his long black hairs on it!" said Tortuga.

"Urgh! Not more!" said Kintana. "That's disgusting! Pa, you could have warned me!"

"Never mind about the hat," said Pa. "What does it say?"

She lay the two pieces of the riddle on the table and read the words aloud

"Only I know
which way to go
Is it east
or west?
My leaves will show."

"It must be a plant of some kind," said Pa. "It mentions leaves."

"It could be leaves in a book," said Tortuga.

"East and west," said Pa, "Why not north and south?"

"It must be an important part of the clue," said Kintana. "A plant used to show east and west . . . Oh, I know! A traveller's palm tree! Their leaves usually grow in an east west direction."

"But there must be hundreds of them on Nosy Boraha, thousands maybe," said Tortuga. "How will you know you are starting in the right spot? Sadly, I'd say your chance of solving the riddle and finding your way to the treasure is wafer thin."

Chapter Twenty

TROUBLE AT THE CROSSROADS

KINTANA AND PA SAID GOODBYE TO THE CAPTAIN and walked back to the pet shop. Kintana felt disheartened as she cleaned out the cages and put in fresh food and water for all the animals.

"We have to find the treasure before Gangrene and Pots," said Kintana, "and try and get the *Curses and Charms* book back before they can use it again."

Pa nodded. "I don't care what the captain says, you've made a good start working out that the leaves must belong to a traveller's palm tree. We're at a crossroads – and I agree, we have to go on."

"Wait! I think that's it! I remember now, there's a traveller's palm tree at the Nosy Boraha crossroads." *Esther had been sat in it. Could that be the one Kidd meant? It would make sense.*

"Then that's where we'll start. At sunrise, we'll take a pirogue across, and check that tree. We should pack . . ."

There was a knock at the door. Kintana jumped. "Oh no! It might be Gangrene and Pots!"

"Who there?" called Pa, lifting up a broom as a weapon.

"It's me, Bartholomew."

Kintana ran to let him in. "Oh! Thank goodness, they've released you." Even his stick insect seemed perkier.

"All thanks to you," he said. "If there's anything I can do as a thank you."

"I don't suppose you could look after the animals, here, for a couple of days?"

Bartholomew chuckled. "Sure, just tell me what I need to do . . ."

☠

Kintana and Pa set off early the next morning. Pa had prepared supplies for their journey including flint and steel, char cloth, rope – as well as food. He filled their knapsacks, then passed one and a water flask to Kintana, before slinging his over his body.

They walked briskly to the Nosy Boraha crossing.

At the water's edge, they dragged out a pirogue and got in.

A loud whistle came from above, and Kintana looked up to see Polly and Esther perched in a guava tree.

"You should get wings like us parrots," suggested Polly – "Much easier."

Kintana giggled.

Pa took the oar and paddled the pirogue to the opposite bank. Then they got out and followed the path to the crossroads. The air smelled of pineapple and cinnamon.

They walked past screw pines with their stilt-like roots – and aromatic clove trees with golden green foliage fringed with pink at the top and heavily scented white flowers.

They reached the crossroads with its four pathways. "There!" Kintana pointed to a tree with a tall trunk topped off with an elaborate fan of paddle-like leaves. She noticed for the first time that several of the leaves weren't glossy and green; they were dried out and brown.

"Some of those leaves look like they don't belong. Polly . . . Esther . . . can you fly up and take a closer look, please?"

The parrots whistled and did as they were asked. "These dead leaves aren't properly attached," called Esther.

"I think someone's stuck them in," said Polly.

"Pull them loose and bring them to me," said Kintana, as Pa took a rest. Propping his wooden leg up on a fallen tree trunk so he could massage his thigh.

The parrots worked quickly, bringing the first dead leaf to her.

Kintana examined the leaf. "Oh! There's something stitched on to the back of this one." The letters were quite small and hard to read . . . it's another riddle!"

> *"Too heavy to fly*
> *long ago it did die*
> *yet its eggs*
> *you may find*
> *where it's dry."*

"Is the answer a parrot?" asked Polly.

"Maybe? *Too heavy to fly* . . . what animals are heavy?" wondered Kintana. "A hippopotamus . . . an elephant . . . a rhinoceros . . ."

"This animal lays eggs though," said Pa. "It must be a bird."

"Oh! I think I know! An elephant bird! There was a feather and some eggshell in Captain Tortuga's collection labelled elephant bird!"

"Well done, you've solved it!" congratulated Pa. "I've heard you can find huge eggs on Madagascar, in the south where it is arid. I doubt there's any on Nosy Boraha, though."

"Check the other leaves in case there's any more riddles," said Esther.

Polly and Esther squawked and flew back up into the traveller's palm tree.

They pulled out the next leaf and brought it to Kintana.

A letter had been painted in a darker green. "It's a clue— *R*. There might be more!" said Kintana, excited.

The parrots flew back to the treetop, fetching her another dried leaf.

"*B*," she said. "These letters might spell out where to go next."

The parrots' routine continued for the next ten minutes.

Kintana lay the leaves out in a row.

R B I E D R V E

"It could be a place name," she said. She moved the letters round.

R E V E D R I B

Pa had a turn. "VE R E B I R D. Perhaps elephant bird is wrong after all!"

Kintana wrinkled her brow. "Let's keep mixing them up." She tried again.

116

"Bed is a word," said Pa.

Kintana grinned. Then looked at the other five letters. "Oh! What if it's not a place, but a geographical feature. "RIVERBED!" she cried. "We need to go to the river." She looked up at the Traveller's Palm Tree. "And now we know which way to go. Not west – because that would take us off back towards Pirate Island. We have to go east!"

"Well, aren't you clever!" said a familiar voice.

Chapter Twenty-One

BIG BUGS

KINTANA GASPED AS GANGRENE STEPPED ON TO the pathway, followed by Pots. The parrots flew off in a panic.

"We've been keepin' an eye on you," said the quartermaster. "We thought you'd come after the treasure now you have our part of the riddle, but we never expected you to come back with *both* parts! And what a bonus, you've even solved the riddle for us! I should have given *you* my three challenges, not Bartholomew."

Kintana bit her lip.

"Gangrene, I don't feel so good!" called Pots. "I feel faint."

"Well, sit down then!" bellowed Gangrene.

Kintana and Pa crept backwards.

Pots sat down on a rotten tree stump. "I need a drink, and food," he panted.

Gangrene rolled his eyes. "There's some berries over there."

"They're too high up," he groaned.

"Stand on that stump under your bum."

Pots grunted, stood up, and rocked the stump back and to. A dozen hissing cockroaches scurried out from under the wood. "Urrgh!" he cried.

"It's only a few bugs," said Gangrene, "don't be a baby."

The hard-shelled brown bugs were crawling over Pots's shoes. "Help! Get them off me!" He kicked out violently but skidded and toppled backwards.

"Leave them alone!" cried Kintana.

Gangrene roared with laughter.

Pots lay on his back, flapping his hands wildly as the cockroaches scuttled over his torso, burrowing into his clothes. Others crawled up his neck and on to his face. Some tried to get into his ears and nose, another scampered towards his eyepatch. Pots screamed, and one fell into his mouth – he spat it out, gasping.

He picked off another from his belly and lobbed it at Gangrene. "See how you like it!"

It landed at the quartermaster's feet – he lifted his shoe and stomped on it.

"Stop it!" cried Kintana, running forward and shoving him backwards.

Gangrene pushed her back, and she landed on her bottom with a bump.

"Get off my daughter!" roared Pa, running over to check she was unhurt.

Kintana pulled herself up. "I said, stop it!" Pa held her back. She squirmed trying to get free.

"She's got more fight in her than you have, Tremblin' Hands," said Gangrene, smirking, until another cockroach ricocheted off his nose.

He spun round. Pots hurled another, and another . . .

Gangrene dodged from side to side. Then he pulled out the *Curses and Charms* book and flicked through the pages. "I've had enough of the lot of you!"

"He's going to do more magic!" Kintana struggled in her pa's grasp.

"This one should be fun!" The quartermaster held the book open so Kintana could see a picture of a man running away from a huge spider. Gangrene bellowed the two words below it. "*Transforma megafauna!*"

A large creaking noise came from the base of the tree. The roots of the screw pine were prizing apart.

Kintana covered her ears – as a monstrously loud, hissing echoed out from the widened gaps.

Two long antennae poked out of from between the roots, followed by a dark head with two bumps on the top.

"It's one of the male cockroaches – but it's huge!" gasped Kintana, backing away.

The super-sized insect was growing rapidly. It was now as big as a lemur.

Gangrene's eyes were wide in admiration. "Look at the size of it; its legs are like a small horse's." He pointed – laughing manically. "Attack!"

The enormous shiny brown bug crawled towards the cook; doubling in size as it neared.

Pots reached for his knife.

But Gangrene has it, realised Kintana.

"Change it back! Please! I'm sorry!" begged Pots, as the male examined his face with its long thin antennae. He tried to fight it off, two arms hopeless against six legs. He fell to the ground and writhed as the cockroach clambered over him.

☙

Now more cockroaches were pushing their way out of the screw pine's roots. There were least ten, all hissing loudly, some with horns, some without.

They were growing rapidly.

"That's it, my beauties," called Gangrene.

The cockroaches waved their antennae towards Kintana and Pa, then charged towards them.

"Run, Kintana!" Pa cried out.

She pulled at his arm. "You, too."

He staggered back, "I'm too slow. Save yourself!"

"Not without you," she pleaded.

Pa began to run, awkwardly.

Kintana glanced back, the cockroaches were right upon them.

She felt a huge, feathery antennae scrape against her head and ducked.

The hissing was terrifying.

Another cockroach flung out a front leg, knocking Pa over. Kintana tried to help him up, but another insect bumped against her with its armour-like shell, and she hit the ground hard.

Kintana gulped as the cockroaches loomed over her.

Chapter Twenty-Two

EGG HUNT

KINTANA CLOSED HER EYES. SHE COULD FEEL more legs and antennae against her skin. "They're just bugs," she told herself. "Really big bugs."

She opened her eyes and stared up at the cockroaches. She'd handled thousands of giant hissing cockroaches in her time. *Just never this giant!*

Kintana pushed herself up. Then stretched out her hands and grabbed the nearest cockroach and tried to twist it round. "Pa, help me."

He grabbed its back legs and thrust. The cockroach was on its way, heading towards Gangrene. Pots was still wrestling with one of the males.

Kintana and Pa reached for the next cockroach and forced it to change direction too.

The quartermaster drew his cutlass. He swung it towards the

first insect, but the blade recoiled off its thick shell. The others had formed a circle round him – they raised their front legs and hissed.

"Quick," whispered Pa. "This is our chance to get away."

Kintana hid her face in his chest as Gangrene slashed again at the cockroach. This time he used his cutlass to flip the creature on to its back. Then he plunged the blade into its abdomen.

Another cockroach went into attack. Gangrene sliced at its legs.

Pa pulled Kintana away and looked into her eyes. "We need to get to the riverbed and find the next clue while they're distracted."

She nodded.

They snuck backwards into the foliage and waded through the long grass and scratching thorns until they could safely re-join the path.

☠

Pa rubbed at his knee above his wooden leg, as they headed for the river. "I wonder if those cockroaches will stay like that. Imagine having some for sale in the shop, we could make a fortune!"

"I don't think there'd be many buyers," laughed Kintana. "And we'd have to build a special paddock for them!"

They walked for an hour until the path split into two directions, north and south. Ahead of them was what must once have been a river but was now completely dried out.

"Somewhere on this old riverbed is our next clue," said Pa. "But it must stretch for miles in both directions. How will we know where to search?"

"Perhaps this is the spot," said Kintana. "Perhaps we have to search here."

She looked down at the dried-up riverbed. It was full of large pebbles and tufted grass. Three dead trees lay in a line, as though they had once been used as stepping stones across the water. Polly and Esther swept into view and landed on one of the trunks.

"Sorry we flew away," said Polly.

Esther snuggled in close to her mate.

"It's all right," said Kintana. "You did the right thing getting to safety. Gangrene put a spell on some hissing cockroaches and turned them into ginormous ones and set them on us and Pots – but we turned them on Gangrene! That's how we got away!"

"Hopefully that's the last we'll see of both of them," said Pa.

"Hmm, hopefully," agreed Kintana. "Right. We need to find the elephant bird egg."

She strode down to the old riverbed.

Pa clambered carefully after her.

Among the pebbles there were a few bigger stones. Kintana lifted them out of the water and checked them, just in case. Occasionally she found one that was particularly egg-shaped, and her heart raced, but it was always another stone.

Pa checked upstream, while Kintana moved downstream. The parrots inspected either side of the bank.

They worked for another half an hour and were now some distance from each other. Kintana paused and took another drink from her flask. The riverbed was starting to bend and if she went much further, she would lose sight of Pa.

Perhaps it would be sensible to go back where they started. She looked downstream and waved at him. "It's hopeless," she called. "We could be looking for hours, days, months! We don't even know that the egg is still here."

"Kidd must have put it somewhere safe," Pa called back. "Let's take a break and eat, while we think about where that may be."

Kintana made her way back and took off her knapsack. Pa gave her his, then they gathered some fresh palm leaves to sit on.

They made a sort of carpet with them, then sat down. Kintana scattered some bird seed on the ground for Polly and Esther. Then she and Pa divided their picnic of dried fish and eel.

Kintana stared at the riverbed as she ate. Was there anything they had missed? What about those three tree trunks where Polly and Esther had landed. *Could they be another clue?*

She finished eating then turned to Pa. "Could you help me roll those trunks over? I'm wondering if there could be another riddle on them, like with the dried leaves."

"Of course," he took a swig from his water flask, and stood up.

Kintana noticed movement in the distance. She put her hand over her eyes, to see clearer in the bright sunlight. "Oh no," she cried. "It's Gangrene and Pots! They must have recovered from the cockroach attack."

"We'd better hurry!" said Pa.

☠

Kintana helped Pa ease himself down on to one knee, so he could balance on his wooden leg.

Then they gripped the first trunk.

"Three, two, one . . ." said Pa – then they pulled.

It rolled over quite easily. Kintana picked up a stone and scraped the mud from the underside. She studied the bark carefully. "Nothing," she sighed.

Kintana could hear a commotion up by the junction. The pirates were pushing and shoving each other. "They're getting closer!"

She and Pa grasped the next trunk and heaved. Kintana scraped again.

Nothing . . . Only one left to check. The third trunk was stuck in the dried-out mud and it took several attempts to get it to roll over.

But at last, it gave. Kintana yelped with joy. She used the stone again to clear the claggy mud.

There was something carved into the wood, some kind of symbol. A rush of excitement coursed through her body. "It's a clue!"

Chapter Twenty-Three

CRACKING CLUES

GANGRENE AND POTS WERE MUCH NEARER NOW! Kintana's heart raced. "Those ovals could be eggs," she said, hurriedly. She peered closer at the carving. "And I think these shapes are meant to be trees with spiders in them!"

"Please, not spiders!" said Pa. "I hate spiders! I don't want to go near any trees with spiders in them!"

"Well, I suppose it could be another creature with eight legs . . . like erm . . ."

"An octopus?" suggested Pa, hopefully.

Kintana giggled. "Only they aren't normally found in trees."

Pa grimaced. "Unlike spiders."

Esther squawked. "So, we're looking for a spider tree, next?"

"Or an octopus tree," said Polly.

"Ha! That's it," said Kintana, clapping her hands. "You've solved the riddle, Polly!"

"Have I?"

"Yes! Over there, look!" She pointed to some tall cactus-like plants a bit further upstream.

"Well, I never!" said Pa, gently slapping her on the back. "Octopus trees! Thank goodness!"

Kintana glanced back at Gangrene and Pots. They were heading down to the riverbed too.

"We've got to get to the next marker before them!" She picked up speed.

Gangrene and Pots began to run.

Kintana and Pa scrambled awkwardly along the riverbed and then up the bank to an area of sandy soil. The parrots flew alongside.

The octopus trees had been planted in a square. They were covered in vicious sharp thorns and each had a crown of green leaves. Kintana stood on tiptoes and could see six large eggs in a large ground nest of twigs and grass on the other side of the spiky barrier. The pirates were getting closer. She had to think quick.

"These cacti don't normally grow on Nosy Boraha," said Pa. "Kidd must have done this."

"The trees must have been planted to stop anyone getting to the eggs," agreed Kintana.

"They won't stop me," said Gangrene as he stumbled towards them. Pots wailing for him to wait.

Pa raised his fists.

Polly and Esther flew higher.

"I'm not afraid of you, Hands. I'm not afraid of anything."

"You were frightened of those cockroaches," scoffed Pa.

"Actually," wheezed Pots, as he crawled up the bank, "once the spell wore off, we squashed every last one of them." He mimicked crushing them underfoot.

Kintana growled. "You shouldn't have done that."

"Oh, shut up, or I'll stomp on you," retorted Pots.

"Now, now," said Gangrene. "Let's be nice, after all Kintana has kindly solved another riddle for us," said Gangrene. "She's led us to the giant eggs."

Pots chortled. "Look at the size of them! I'd like to boil one of them for my breakfast!"

"You're not getting your filthy hands on them," said Kintana, folding her arms.

"Ha! Yes, we are." Gangrene pulled out the *Curses and Charms* book from his bag. "I only need the right spell to make those eggs float over that prickly cacti and I will have the next clue."

"Squawk!!!!" Polly swooped down on Gangrene and pecked at his arms and head.

"You mangy fleabag. I'll have your beak off!" He drew his cutlass. Polly flew higher.

I have to stop him! thought Kintana. There was no way to get the book off Gangrene, not while he had his cutlass. But perhaps she could use one of the spells herself?

Will it work without the book? And can I remember the words correctly? Kintana hoped so, she pointed her finger at the parrot. "*Transforma Megafauna!*"

A flash of light shot towards the bird as Gangrene raised his cutlass again. Esther knocked Polly aside, taking the full force of the spell, a bright light showering the octopus trees and nest.

Esther's body sparkled with light as she spiralled slowly to the ground.

"Oh no!" Kintana ran to Esther, tears welling – the parrot's feathers were singed, smoke rose off her yellow head. She glanced over at Pa for help, but he was still wrestling Pots.

"Ha! You killed her," gloated Gangrene. "One down, one to go." He slashed his cutlass again at Polly, who was still swooping at the pirate.

Kintana crouched. "*Esther.*"

The parrot's eyes fluttered open. "What happened?"

"I'm so sorry! I was trying to cast a growth spell so Polly could attack Gangrene. I didn't know what else to do!"

"I feel strange," muttered Esther, as her feathers started to shimmer again. Her talons were growing – her feet and her legs too. Kintana watched as Esther changed. She was the size of a hen, then a turkey, then a swan . . .

Pots and Pa had stopped fighting; they both stood, staring.

Polly gave a squawk. "She's enormous!"

Gangrene clutched the spell book to his chest and swung his cutlass again, catching the end of a tail feather.

Polly squawked once more and soared up high into a tall rosewood tree. He hid deep in its branches, out of reach of the quartermaster's cutlass.

"Esther! You've got to scare off Gangrene and Pots before the spell wears off," Kintana pleaded.

The female vasa parrot was now as tall as an ostrich! "I can't attack now!" she squawked. "I've got to look after the eggs!"

"The eggs can wait, Esther," said Kintana. "You have to frighten the pirates away!"

Esther ruffled her feathers. "But they're about to hatch!" She turned round and hopped with ease over the octopus trees.

Kintana looked to the brood. *Surely the eggs can't hatch. They must be over a hundred years old.* Her jaw dropped; the eggs were shimmering strangely too! *Has the magic affected them as well?*

Esther gently lowered herself onto the nest. "I have to keep them warm."

There was a slow, cracking noise and the sulphuric smell of rotten eggs.

Esther stood up and tucked her head between her legs.

A jagged line appeared around the centre of each egg.

"My babies are ready!"

Kintana could see an egg tooth pecking away at one, and soon she got glimpses of sticky, wet feathers, then a wing, a leg.

The chicks pushed apart the shell and began to chirp.

"Aren't they beautiful," said Esther proudly, as they were fully revealed.

Their brown feathers were still sticky as they began to preen themselves with a beak that reminded Kintana of a shovel's blade.

They tried to stand, on thick, muscular legs, stretching their long necks as they started to grow.

Kintana stepped back, as the chicks' bodies ballooned, just as Esther's had done. Only the elephant birds were already as big as an ostrich and still growing.

They towered over their adoptive mother.

"Attack my darlings," Esther pointed her wing at Gangrene, then Pots.

The chicks were wobbly at first, as they got to their feet. One was bigger than the others! It was twice the height of the pirates! It made a loud cry, then trampled over the octopus trees, crushing them underfoot.

The big chick's brothers and sisters stumbled after their sibling making a sinister guttural vibrating sound.

Pa shoved Pots, right into the path of the first elephant bird chick – which trod on his feet.

"Aargh!" the cook moaned, dropping on to his bottom and clutching his toes. "It's broken them!"

Gangrene laughed, but his amusement was short lived as the sibling birds turned to face him.

Pots cheered, "Get him!" as they trundled towards the quartermaster.

They backed Gangrene up against a palm tree.

Kintana watched as the biggest chick darted its long neck again and again at the spell book, trying to jab it with its beak.

Gangrene jerked the book out of reach. Then dived between the bird's legs and sprinted along the riverbed.

The remaining birds gave chase.

"Come back!" cried Pots. "I need the dokotera!"

The largest bird swung around and stomped towards the cook.

"Help! Help!" Pots tried to get up, weeping with pain. "Gangrene!"

The elephant bird jabbed down and clamped its beak around Pot's collar and lifted him off the ground.

Pots flapped and kicked, as the elephant bird carried him off up the bank towards the trees.

"Well done, my babies!" called Esther, as his screams became quieter and quieter.

Kintana and Pa stood in shock for a moment. Then they tread carefully over the flattened octopus trees to get to the remains of the elephant bird eggs. They picked up each piece, in turn, and scrutinised them for markings.

Then Kintana spotted the top of a whole egg poking out of the ground. She carefully scooped away the dirt to reveal a whole egg.

As she picked it up, it came apart in two halves. There were words inked onto the inside of the shell.

> *"Don't stall*
> *it's time to crawl*
> *to pass*
> *through*
> *the waterfall."*

Kintana put the eggshell into her knapsack. "Which way?"

Esther waved a shrinking wing upstream. Her feathers twinkling all over as the magic wore off.

Chapter Twenty-Four

ANGRY WORDS

AFTER ABOUT AN HOUR THEY ENTERED THE Ikalalao forest. The trees were denser here, their lush leaves providing some much-needed shade. Kintana could hear lemurs in the canopy and in the distance, the sound of water was getting louder and louder.

There were orchids everywhere. A large swallowtail butterfly fluttered past.

Pa was getting slower and Kintana worried his knee was rubbing painfully against his wooden leg. They paused to collect some guava fruit for later.

Eventually the riverbed joined with a wide, fast-flowing river. It stretched out in front of them.

"Let's refill our flasks," said Kintana. "And I want to re-read the third riddle." She reached into her bag and pulled out the two parts of the eggshell, putting them together.

They settled on a couple of boulders at the river's edge. Polly and Esther perched beside them.

Kintana read the riddle aloud again. "*Don't stall, it's time to crawl to pass through the waterfall.*"

"What's that? Another clue to the treasure!" Gangrene staggered on to the path. He'd lost his bandana and his hair had been tugged out of its plait. There was a muddy bird footprint on the cover of the *Curses and Charms* book, in his hand.

"Not you again," moaned Kintana, standing up.

"Don't you ever give up," moaned Polly. "Why couldn't those overgrown chickens have eaten you."

"If I get my hands on you it'll be roast parrot for my tea," snarled Gangrene. "I'm sick of your wisecracks."

"Where's Pots?" asked Kintana.

Gangrene shrugged. "Don't know. Don't care."

A howl came from the trees behind them.

"What was *that*?" asked Kintana.

"Sounds like somethin' mean, big and ferocious," said Gangrene, menacingly. "Somethin' that probably likes to devour little girls. Now, hand over that eggshell."

"Never!" said Kintana.

"We're not afraid of you," said Pa, standing.

Gangrene grabbed the eggshell, read the words quickly, then threw the two halves on the floor and stamped up and down on them.

"You're just a bully," said Esther.

"No wonder Snuffles ran away," added Polly.

Gangrene growled. "You mouthy little pigeon. I'm goin' to make you shut up once and for all!" He opened the *Curses and*

Charms book and stabbed at a picture of a chameleon with its long tongue stretched out. There were two words underneath it. "Ha! This one should silence you! . . . he raised his voice, "*Lingua linger!*"

Polly squawked in horror, and dodged a blast of white light, just in time. The forest behind him lit up.

Kintana ran forward. "Polly, are you all right?"

Gangrene grabbed her. "You'll be next!"

She kicked at his ankles and tried to wriggle free.

"Let her go," cried Pa, about to rush forward.

But something was bounding towards them, flattening down all vegetation in its path.

Pa halted. Kintana screamed.

Polly and Esther squawked.

A blur of golden brown leapt out and sent Gangrene flying backwards.

It was a fossa!

"Whiskers!" cried Polly.

"Help, help," cried Gangrene, as the fossa tore at him. He rolled over and over in a struggle with the carnivore, its jaw clamped tight round the pirate's weapon arm.

Kintana sobbed, "Stop!"

The fossa released its grip and turned to face her. "Hate man. Kill man," it spat.

Chapter Twenty-Five

CHOICES

KINTANA RUBBED HER EARS AND STARED AT THE fossa. "Whiskers! You spoke!"

Gangrene cowered on the floor, his clothes torn, his skin dripping blood.

The fossa stretched its back. "Hunt in forest. Hunt giant jumping rat. Hear Bad Man. Light hit."

"The spell," said Polly, "it missed me, it must have struck Whiskers!"

"Yes, and Gangrene made a mistake," said Kintana. "That spell doesn't silence someone – it gives them power of speech!"

"Leave Man. Be Free."

The fossa stared at Kintana.

Her heart thudded.

"Girl good. Girl release Whiskers."

"Whiskers Go. Live in Forest," said Kintana, wondering if this spell would also wear off.

Whisker's eyes glinted. "First Find master. Hate master." She flicked her long tail, then bounded away.

"Great, a talking fossa" said Polly, "I can't stand talking animals!"

Kintana and Pa dragged a dishevelled Gangrene up against a tree.

"We should go back to *The Nine Sails* and get help for him and Pots," said Kintana.

"Should we? You wanted to be a pirate, Kintana. What would a pirate do?"

She grinned. "A pirate would go after the treasure."

"We'll stay and keep an eye on Gangrene," said Polly.

"And make sure Pots isn't still following," added Esther.

"We'll tie him up to make sure," said Pa, wrenching *Curses and Charms* away from Gangrene.

He passed the spell book to Kintana and took a rope from his knapsack.

"We'd better take Pots's knife too," she delved into Gangrene's bag and fished out the blade.

"I'll have my revenge for this," Gangrene snarled, as Pa wound the rope around him.

"I don't think so," said Pa. "We'll send word to *The Nine Sails* once we have the treasure. Captain Tortuga will have you and Pots thrown in the dungeon at the old fort."

Gangrene grunted.

"Come on, let's go," said Pa.

Kintana said goodbye to the parrots, then followed Pa.

☠

They walked along the river's edge. There was no path now, and it was uneven underfoot.

"I hate to say it, but I don't think we're going to make it to the waterfall before dark," said Pa, an hour later. "I think we need to look for somewhere to camp overnight. We'd better start making a shelter."

He took out Gangrene's knife and headed into the forest.

Kintana started gathering leaves.

Pa returned a short while later with an armful of long, thick, branches – stripped of their leaves.

Together they interlocked the branches to make a basic triangular structure. Their hands were soon smeared with dirt.

Happy with the shape's sturdiness they added in more smaller branches, thickening the walls. Then it was time to make the roof waterproof in case the weather turned overnight.

Kintana scooped together her leaves and weaved them between the branches, then added more to the floor inside.

"Fire next," said Pa. It was essential for heat and light, and it would also keep biting insects at bay.

Pa searched the ground for fallen branches, the older, the better. Big, dry, pieces of wood that would burn for a long time. While Kintana gathered kindling – thinner sticks that would help build heat.

Pa found four heavy, thick branches and dragged them into a square to create a firebreak.

Kintana piled the firewood in the centre of the firebreak, leaving room for air to circulate underneath.

Pa added smaller branches, while Kintana looked for twigs and dried grass to use as tinder.

Everything in place, Pa placed some char cloth on the tinder, then struck his flint and steel. The spark caught and soon the fire was burning nicely.

Kintana liked the smell, but the drifting smoke irritated her eyes.

She flicked through the *Curses and Charms* book looking at all the spells. "I was right, Gangrene used the wrong *lingua* spell – *linger* doesn't silence people, it lets them speak in any language. – To silence Polly he should have said *mutio*."

"Polly had a very lucky escape," said Pa. "Thank goodness Gangrene won't be castin' any more spells."

Kintana passed the book to Pa. "You'd better put it in your knapsack for safekeeping."

They ate the last of their dried fish then shared out the guava fruit.

They refilled their water bottles from the river. Then crawled into their shelter, hoping for a good night's sleep.

☠

Kintana awoke to the sounds of the forest. Lemurs were calling somewhere in the distance, and she thought she could hear the faint sound of rushing water.

She gathered up their belongings while Pa checked the fire was safely extinguished.

They set off, refreshed, admiring the beauty of the forest. There were pitcher plants, comet orchids, vines and lianas.

They stepped over tree roots and skirted round muddy sections – the sound of the waterfall getting louder with every step, until it roared like thunder.

They walked quicker now. Until they could finally see the waterfall ahead of them.

Torrents of white water cascaded over thick granite, into the river below.

Kintana lowered herself down the bank, Pa close behind. She wiped spray from her face and eased herself across the mossy stone to get closer to the waterfall, her ears ringing from the constant sound.

Through the curtain of water, Kintana could see that the granite was the opening to a hidden cave. She gripped the rocks and moved slowly closer, being careful not to slip.

The water pelted her head as she stepped into the gap behind. She shook her hair and waited for her eyes to adjust to the dark.

The air was damp and musty. Pa stepped into the cave after her. "Phew, made it." He opened his bag and took out two candles. He lit them, then passed one to Kintana. "We need to go slow, so they don't blow out."

Kintana could see the way ahead split into two passages. "Which do we choose?"

Chapter Twenty-Six

DECOY

THE TWO TUNNEL ENTRANCES LOOKED IDENTICAL. Kintana lifted her candle and checked the rock around them for markings.

There was nothing above the left one. She moved to the right one. There was a faintly scratched drawing of a chest. "This one," she said, confidently.

"Wait," he said. "What if Pots or Gangrene are still followin'? We need to hide this clue." Pa reached into his bag and pulled out the cook's knife, then scraped at the rock, removing all traces of the chest. "Can you draw a chest above the other passage?" he asked, offering the knife.

"I'll try."

She gripped the handle and scratched out a rectangle with a semi-circular lid.

"Perfect." He put the knife away.

"I'll go first," said Kintana, crouching. "I'm smaller than you." She crawled into the tunnel, holding her candle.

A small group of mouse lemurs blinked their huge orange eyes at her, then scurried away.

The ground was rough on her hand and knees, but after a short distance it curved and became much wider. Kintana rubbed her neck and straightened up. "Pa! Can you hear me?" Her voice echoed.

"Yes!"

"The tunnel starts narrow, but then it opens up. You'll be fine . . ."

"As long as there's no spiders!"

She listened to Pa shuffling along the passage, the light from his candle getting brighter as he neared.

"That was hard work," he said. "I'm puffed."

Pa was limping slightly, as they continued on.

At last, they came to the end of the tunnel.

A large, round cavern stretched out before them. The top of the cavern had collapsed, but a few stalactites and tree roots encircled the large roof hole.

There were several more passages leading away from the cavern, like cogs on a wheel. *I wonder where they lead*, thought Kintana.

She reached out to touch one of the milky white stalagmites, that looked like melted wax; it was cold and wet.

The walls were covered in ancient paintings; muted reds and faded whites depicting giant lemurs with long arms and legs and cute round faces. They were hanging from the branches of huge trees, their limbs arcing over many other creatures. A huge bird, small hippopotamuses and a large lemur as big as a gorilla. Above them was a magnificent eagle, its wings spread wide on a gentle breeze.

Kintana knew this was a snapshot of a former time in Madagascar, before these wonderful animals were driven into extinction.

"This is true treasure, isn't it, Pa?" realised Kintana. "These paintings. The cave."

"Yes, but it's not the treasure that Gangrene and Pots are after."

"Do you think this is where the chest is hidden?" she asked.

She looked round the rest of the cave, checking the rest of the walls. Nothing.

Kintana sighed and sat on a lump of rock. She dropped her head, feeling weary. "Oh!" There was something scratched into the rock by her feet. She giggled as she read the words to Pa.

"No time for a rest
you must finish the quest
Climb up
to find the
treasure chest."

Pa clapped. "I'll lift you to one of those vines and then you pull yourself up."

Kintana hurried to one of the lowest hanging vines and grabbed it. She pulled herself up, gripping tightly. It was even harder than climbing the rigging to get to the crow's nest.

Suddenly, a cloud of leathery-winged tomb bats burst out of the other tunnel. Kintana yelped, nearly slipping with shock. The mouse lemurs scurried back into their passageway as the bats flew through the gaping hole.

"Careful, Kintana!" called Pa.

Kintana stretched out her hand and pushed up again. The roof seemed so far away. "If I can do it, so can you, Pa."

He laughed. "Fair enough." He looked for a thicker vine and started to climb up after her.

His wooden leg made it even harder for him. "Good job I've got strong arm muscles from all those years climbin' riggin'."

She looked down. "Watch out! Your bag's open," but it was too late – the *Curses and Charms* book slipped out and fell to the ground.

"I'll go back for it!"

"No, Pa. You'll be exhausted. We can come back for it once we have the treasure. Then we can destroy it once and for all."

He nodded.

Kintana pushed on. The light was getting brighter, the air fresher. At last, she was through the roof; she scrambled over the edge and collapsed on the moist grass.

She glanced up and gasped. In front of her was an enormous ivory treasure chest covered in colourful jewels!

A circle of maki – ring-tailed lemurs – were sitting guard around the chest and right on top of the chest was sat a large black-and-white babakoto, the biggest of all the lemurs. It opened its mouth and made its eerie, ghost-like call.

Pa pulled himself up through the roof into the forest. Then cheered. "We did it!"

Kintana grinned. The chest was encrusted with blue sapphires and turquoise, green emeralds and jade, yellow diamonds and red rubies.

"Captain Kidd must have brought these lemurs here from the

mainland to guard his treasure," whispered Kintana to Pa, as she reached into her pocket for leftover guava fruit. She crept forward, holding the food at arm's length.

The maki sniffed the air, then one of the females reached out and took the offering.

It passed it back to the babakoto, which seemed to be in charge.

"I can see a padlock," Kintana whispered, as she edged back to Pa, "but there's no keyhole."

"How do you open a lock without a key?" he asked.

"Magic?" Kintana sucked her lips together.

"I knew I should have gone back down for the Curses and Charms book," said Pa, with a sigh.

"Don't worry, I can get it," said Kintana.

Suddenly, the maki stood on their hind legs and began to call out in alarm.

The babakoto howled.

Kintana turned round.

"Too late!" said Gangrene, clambering out of the cavern roof. "I already have it. That treasure is mine!"

Chapter Twenty-Seven

THE TREASURE CHEST

"YOU SHOULD HAVE LET YOUR DAUGHTER TIE ME up. Your knot skills aren't what they were," gloated Gangrene, drawing his cutlass.

Kintana clung to Pa. She couldn't believe he'd caught up with them again. *His injuries can't have been as bad as we thought.*

Gangrene strode past them and towards the treasure chest. "I can only imagine the bounty inside. Gold. Silver. Pearls. Precious Jewels. I'm going to live like a Sultan!"

The babakoto climbed off the chest and stood in front of the padlock.

"I'm not afraid of a few mangy monkeys," said Gangrene, yet he moved no further.

"They're *lemurs*," snapped Kintana, "not monkeys, you ignoramus."

"No need to be rude! Just because you're angry that you led me to the treasure."

"What have you done with Polly and Esther?" Kintana demanded.

"Nothing," Gangrene wiped his nose on the back of his hand. "When I woke up, they'd gone. The cowards must have flown away."

"I don't believe you."

Gangrene shrugged. "I don't care," he retorted. He opened the *Curses and Charms* book, then hesitated as the maki bared their teeth.

Gangrene flicked through the pages of *Curses and Charms*. "Now I only need to find the right spell to open that padlock."

Kintana clenched her fists. "You're not going to get away with this."

"That's right," said a new voice.

Captain Tortuga stepped out of the forest. Polly and Esther were perched on his shoulders. "These parrots have told me everything."

"Oh, thank goodness!" said Kintana. "You're just in time. Gangrene is about to take the treasure."

"Don't worry, child," he smiled. "I have no intention of letting him near MY treasure!"

"Your treasure?" spluttered Gangrene.

"Yes, MY treasure. Do you think I'm an idiot, Mr Gangrene? I've known about your treasure hunting plans all along." He drew his pistol and pointed it at Gangrene.

Polly and Esther squawked and took flight.

Pa shielded Kintana.

"Don't be hasty!" said Gangrene, raising his hands. "I'm willing to share."

Tortuga waved his gun, forcing Gangrene away from the chest.

"I don't even expect half," the quartermaster continued. "I'll be satisfied with a quarter of the booty. Honest!"

"But I'm not sharing," Tortuga replied. And with that he fired his pistol.

Gangrene hit the ground, the *Curses and Charms* book falling from his limp hand.

Kintana screamed. "You've killed him!"

Captain Tortuga took off his hat and wiped his brow. "Oh, Kintana, haven't you learned yet that pirates are lying, cheating, double-crossing thieves. I always meant to kill Gangrene and Pots as soon as they led me here. Poor chaps. I quite enjoyed their pathetic attempt to put me in a trance . . ." He laughed.

"Attempt?" repeated Kintana.

"I was only *pretending* to be under their spell. I've been pretending all along. Pretending that I didn't know Gangrene was planning a mutiny, pretending I didn't know you were a girl . . ."

Kintana's blood ran cold. Captain Tortuga had completely fooled her. *I trusted him.*

"I knew they had Blackbeard's head in a jar in the galley – a captain knows every inch of his ship – but the head alone was no good to them. They had to resurrect him, if they were going to find the other half of Kidd's riddle." He strode over to the quartermaster and picked up the Curses and Charms book.

"How do you think Gangrene knew about this book in the first place? I told him about it, of course. Then, once we'd left Pirate Island, I put it in my desk drawer with the aye-aye finger for him to steal."

The aye-aye finger! She'd forgotten all about it. Kintana slipped her hand into her pocket. This time she felt relief. It was still there.

"Of course things got complicated when he involved that foolish boy, but I played along with that ridiculous attempt at a mutiny. And with all my cards in place, so to speak, I could play my final hand. The stolen flag meant we would return to Pirate Island for the trial – then I simply had to bide my time while Gangrene and Pots resurrected Blackbeard.

"Now there's only you two to deal with." He began flicking through the pages of Curses and Charms.

It's all my fault! realised Kintana. *I've led Tortuga to the chest. Pots is missing and Gangrene is dead, and now Tortuga's going to kill me and Pa.*

All because she'd wanted an adventure, to be a pirate so she could show Pa she was growing up.

I must stop Tortuga! Kintana clasped the aye-aye finger tighter. *Will it even work now it's broken?*

If she could resurrect Gangrene, would he help her and Pa, or choose to side with his captain?

"The treasure will be mine again!" proclaimed Tortuga.

"Never!" cried Kintana. She pulled out the broken aye-aye finger and clamped the two pieces together.

Chapter Twenty-Eight

BROKEN

KINTANA TURNED THE BROKEN FINGER THREE times, but it was impossible to keep the pieces together and make complete turns. She looked to the skies, there were no gathering clouds. Gangrene was still lying on the ground.

Kintana stared at the broken pieces in her hand and collapsed into Pa's chest, weeping.

Captain Tortuga laughed. "The aye-aye finger won't work any more, not snapped in two. You're not worth bothering with, you're as pathetic as your pa."

He strode towards the chest, his hand in front of him. "*Unsealio Curiosio.*"

The babakoto leapt off the lid as the padlock shankle slackened. The front of the chest had transformed so it opened at the front like a cupboard.

Tortuga removed the open padlock and tossed it aside. "Of

course, Gangrene and Pots misunderstood the nature of my treasure. This is not a treasure chest in the traditional sense. It is a cabinet of curiosities. Curiosities with great power." He opened the doors revealing shelves crammed with glass specimen jars.

Kintana and Pa shuffled forward.

"As I already told Kintana, I've spent a lifetime collecting. I'm fascinated by animals. I've studied them in life and death. I have collected poisons from snakes and frogs. I have eaten tiger and lion to make me strong. I've dissected chameleons to find out their power to change colour so I could learn the art of camouflage. And I bought Plank, my giant tortoise, so I could discover the secret of a long life."

Kintana felt sick.

Tortuga held a jar aloft. "I put all the organs and skin and teeth in preserving liquid to retain their potency. Then I put the jars in my cabinet so no one else could have them." He wiped his brow and caressed its cool ivory surface. "But still I craved more knowledge. So, I interrogated medicine men, Malagasy ombiasa, witch doctors – and shamen. I demanded them to tell me about the magical properties of animals, long forgotten curses and charms. I wrote all that knowledge down in this book. With my cabinet I was ready to use my power and become the most fearsome pirate that ever sailed."

"What went wrong?" asked Pa.

"Kidd, the Pirate Hunter, he came after me, attacked my ship and confiscated all my possessions, including my cabinet. The fool presumed it was filled with gold and jewels, just like Gangrene and Pots." He put the jar down. "Fortunately, the only things Kidd wasn't interested in were my animals and my books.

"Then in a twist of fate, Kidd became the hunted. I sat through the trial in London, in futile hope that I would learn the whereabouts of my chest. But at least I got the pleasure of watching Kidd's execution."

Kintana shook her head. The captain was a truly wicked man.

"They strung Kidd up next to three others at the gallows. When they pulled the blocks away, the hanging rope snapped, and Kidd dropped to the ground. He must have thought his survival was an act of god. Perhaps they'd even pardon him." Tortuga laughed. "They didn't, they got a fresh noose and made him climb the steps again!

"They preserved Kidd's corpse with tar and swung it in a gibbet from a post by the River Thames as a warning to other pirates. That made me feel better for a short while . . .

"Still, it has all turned out well in the end, thanks to you Kintana. I will return to *The Nine Sails* with my cabinet and I will rule the seas with my cowering crew as my slaves!"

He took off his hat and wiped his brow.

Suddenly Polly and Esther swooped overhead and released a trail of bird poo over the captain.

"Urrghh! You dirty beasts!" cried Tortuga, as sticky white mess dripped down his face.

Kintana pointed her index finger at Tortuga. "*Lingua Mutio!*"

The captain's mouth opened in a roar but not a sound came out of his mouth. He could not cast any more spells. His body shook with fury.

She had two more spells to cast.

"*Sealio Curiosio!*" Kintana grinned as the chest doors slammed shut and the padlock clinked back together.

She pointed at herself "*Lingua linger!*"

Tortuga's eyes were wide with anger. He tore at the padlock.

Kintana's head filled with new thoughts, sounds and language. Her tongue and lips formed new shapes and sounds.

She spoke to the babakoto first, telling him all about Tortuga's evil ways, appealing for his help. The lemur howled at the captain and slammed its hands down on the chest.

The maki swished their black-and-white tails – they raised their arms and began an alarm call.

Kintana cupped her hands around her mouth and joined in with the holler, summoning more lemurs.

"She's not loud enough alone," said Pa. "We have to help." He pointed at himself. "*Lingua linger!*"

Polly and Esther pointed a wing at each other. "*Lingua linger!*"

Together they howled and wailed alongside Kintana and the lemurs.

Tortuga froze as the air was filled with replies.

"It's working!" Kintana cheered, as hundreds more lemurs dropped down from the canopy. She had never seen so many different types in one place. There were creamy sifaka, black-and-white-ruffed, red-ruffed, red-bellied, brown, black, dwarf, crowned and more maki and babakoto.

They all charged at Tortuga, shrieking wildly.

He screamed, noiselessly, and staggered back towards the edge of the cavern. He fell to his knees and grabbed at the vine, then lowered himself over the side.

Kintana and Pa rushed to see. They crouched and peered over. She didn't want to see Gangrene's body, so she focused on the vine. Tortuga was descending with ease and skill.

"We have to stop him from getting away!" she said.

Below the vine, hundreds of eyes blinked up at her. *The mouse lemurs! Can they help?* Kintana called to them in their language.

They chirped back. "They say they're too small to stop him," she clutched Pa's hand. "but they're going to ask for help."

Tortuga dropped to the ground, and the little creatures scattered.

"Kintana!" cried Polly and Esther.

She spun round to see two giant sloth lemurs swing out of the canopy. They were massive! Perhaps the aye-aye finger had summoned the dead back to life – as these lemurs had been extinct for thousands of years!

They used their long limbs to propel themselves from the end of branches down into the cavern.

The giant sloth lemurs landed with a thud either side of Tortuga then, with a quick flick of their hook-like claws, they pulled him on to his back.

"Aarrgghh!" Tortuga flailed like an upturned cockroach, helpless against the creature's strength.

The giant sloth lemurs dragged the captain towards one of the passages before disappearing into the darkness, the mouse lemurs scurrying after them.

"He's gone," said Kintana. She felt her body relax.

"Wait," called Pa. "What's that?" He pointed into the overgrowth.

"Snuffles!" Kintana cried.

The giant jumping rat leaped across the ground, towards his master.

She felt strangely sad. Though Gangrene had been horrible, she hadn't wished him dead.

Snuffles was at the quartermaster's side, his whiskers softly caressing his face,

There was a quiet moan.

"He's not dead!" gasped Kintana.

"What?" said Pa. "Impossible! Let me check." He hurried over to Gangrene, pulling back his waistcoat to look at his injury. He gasped. "There's no blood!"

Gangrene's eyes flickered open. Snuffles rubbed his face against his cheek.

"Tortuga must have missed! There's not a mark on him!"

"Gangrene must have fainted in terror!" laughed Kintana. "You'd better let me tie him up this time. But first we have to hide the treasure chest."

She held the aye-aye finger out to one of the maki.

The lemurs gathered around the chest.

"Hide the chest," she told them in their language, already finding she was losing the ability to translate her words.

The lemurs raised their arms and hollered one last time, then together, they pushed the chest into the forest.

"It's for the best," said Kintana.

Chapter Twenty-Nine

REWARDS

POLLY AND ESTHER SWOOPED ONTO KINTANA'S shoulders. "Weren't we great!" they squawked.

"The greatest vasa parrots ever!" replied Kintana with a grin.

Esther shook out a few more yellow feathers. "What an adventure we've had! Pickled heads, resurrected pirate skeletons, elephant birds . . . it's a wonder I've any feathers left at all!"

Kintana laughed, she had always thought she had to travel to find adventure and yet she'd found one close to home. She sat down, feeling exhausted. "Ouch!" She lifted her bottom and reached under with her hand. There was something sharp on the ground.

She brushed through the grass, her fingers clasping something hard.

Kintana picked it up. It shone green in the sunlight.

It was a huge emerald!

"Booty!" squawked Polly, as Kintana turned the jewel round and round in her hand. "Are there any others?"

Kintana and Pa began to search.

She felt something else. Her heart was racing. "A ruby!"

"Uggh, a spider and it's huge!" cried Pa, holding up a tiny arachnid.

"Don't be silly," teased Kintana.

The parrots joined in with the hunt.

"A diamond!" declared Esther, rolling it out of the grass with her beak.

"And a topaz," added Polly.

Pa thrust his hand in the air. "I've got a sapphire!"

"They must have fallen off the treasure chest.," added Kintana, scooping up a large purple amethyst. "Do you think we can keep these?"

"We deserve a reward, don't we?" replied Pa.

Kintana grinned. "We do!"

"Imagine how much bird seed you can buy!" said Polly.

Pa laughed. "You can both have as much seed and crackers as you like for the rest of your lives. Now let's head back to *The Nine Sails* so you can sail on to your next adventure!"

Kintana nodded – but even with the fading power of the *lingua linger* spell, she couldn't think of anything to say.

She had wanted so desperately to be a pirate. She had craved excitement and thrills and got far more than she could ever have expected. *But do I really want a life at sea drinking dirty grog and eating stale tack? Attacking ships and stealing. Never knowing when I'll see home again.*

The following evening, they arrived back on Pirate Island. Polly and Esther flew circles round Kintana and Pa, as they crossed the gangplank on to *The Nine Sails*.

Croak, Spike, Zachariah and Bartholomew rushed forward to greet them.

"Did you find Kidd's treasure?" asked Bartholomew.

"Or did Gangrene and Pots get to it first?" asked Spike.

"Slow down, you two, or you'll trip over your tongues," replied Pa. "We'll tell you everythin', once we've had somethin' proper to eat and drink."

"Are the pets all right?" asked Kintana.

"Oh, yes," said Bartholomew. "I've really enjoyed looking after them."

Pa slapped him on the back. "Well done."

His cheeks burned bright red.

"Now, let's all go to the galley and I'll tell you the whole story," said Pa. "You won't believe your ears! We'll need to send some gravediggers to do some tidying up at the pirate cemetery . . ."

The pirates looked at each other, intrigued.

"And I'll need some volunteers to bring back Pots and Gangrene to Pirate Island, they've both had a bit of an accident over on Nosy Boraha," Pa added.

Bartholomew's eyes were as wide as a Madagascan Owl's!

"I'm going to stay up on deck," said Kintana. "I need some air."

Pa frowned. "All right. If you're sure. I'll shout you when dinner is ready."

✷

Half an hour later, Kintana was shaken from her thoughts by her name being called again and again.

"Kintana!"

"Kintana!"

"Is it true?" asked Croak, his eyes bulging like his pet frog's. "About the spells and the mad monkeys."

"Lemurs," corrected Kintana softly, "Yes, it's true."

"And is it true Captain Tortuga was planning to turn us all into 'is slaves?" asked Zachariah.

"Yes, that's true too."

"Kintana! You must be the best pirate EVER!" said Bartholomew.

"You should be our new captain," said Spike.

"Yes, three cheers for Captain Kintana," cried Zachariah.

"Well?" asked Pa. "How does that sound to you?"

"Me? Captain of *The Nine Sails*?" It was amazing, flattering, surely a dream come true. So why did it feel like the worst idea ever?

"We should celebrate!" cried Pa before she could say any more. He threw his arms round her. "We need food, and music."

The pirates didn't need telling twice. They gathered barrels of rum and grog and all kinds of delicious food.

One crew member had a pole across his shoulders with a huge bunch of bananas hanging from each side. Kintana grabbed one then walked across the deck, looking for a quiet spot to sit. The place was in chaos, with nowhere to get away. She sighed – until she spotted Polly and Esther soaring around the crow's nest. Climbing it was much easier third time around.

The platform had a bird's eye view of the celebrations. Down below the pirates were having a fantastic time.

They had lit lanterns and strung them across the masts. *The*

Nine Sails looked especially pretty as the sky darkened with nightfall.

She closed her eyes and listened to the now familiar sounds of waves splashing against wood and the ship's creaks and groans. Someone had started singing a sea shanty.

Everyone was in a great mood. Everyone except Kintana.

Polly and Esther swooped over again and then landed next to her.

"Why are you hiding up here?" asked Polly. "Ooh, is that banana?"

Kintana grinned and offered him a piece.

"Pirate Island is a pretty special place, isn't it?" said Kintana.

"That's because it's your home. You don't need to sail the seas to know home is where the heart is."

"You're right, Polly. You really are very clever! I'm going to go down now. I need to find my pa."

Kintana descended quickly, then ran across the deck. "Pa! Pa!" she called.

Then, there he was. She threw her arms out and ran to him, hugging him as hard as she could. "I want to come home, Pa. I don't want to be a captain. I don't even want to be a pirate. I love animals. Just like you. I want to care for them and protect them. Not just the ones in the shop, but all the ones on the island too."

"Well, that is good news!" said Pa with a wink. "Because I've just told the crew I'd give Plank a permanent home and I understand you're really good at walking him."

"And what about all the other animals that Tortuga kept. Can't we help them too?"

"Oh, Kintana, I'd like too, but there are so many."

"We could convert *The Nine Sails* – turn her into a floating pet shop! You would be in charge – after all a ship needs a captain! We can sail around Madagascar protecting the wildlife all along the coast."

"And what about the pirates?" asked Pa. "They might not like the idea."

"If they don't they can sign articles with other ships," she said with a shrug, "though hopefully some of them might want to stay and help us." Kintana was looking at Bartholomew. He was a bit stupid sometimes, but his heart was in the right place. "Especially when they learn what a good cook you are!"

"Will there be room for a couple of parrots?" asked Esther.

"We'd be no trouble at all," said Polly.

"We've always got room for a couple of parrots at Pirate Island Pet Shop. Only I think we should give the ship a new name." Kintana was picturing herself up a ladder giving a new sign a clean. "Let's call it The Nine *Tails* Pet Emporium!"

GLOSSARY

✸ **Articles**: A contract signed by a ship's new crew member. Includes rules of behaviour.

✸ **Babakoto**: Malagasy name for Indri, a large black and white lemur.

✸ **Backstaff**: a navigational instrument used to measure the sun's height above sea water from its shadow.

✸ **Ballast**: heavy material – such as gravel, sand, or iron – placed in the hull of a ship to ensure its stability.

✸ **Berth**: A bunk – a place to sleep on a ship.

✸ **Betsimisaraka**: Madagascar has eighteen different ethnic groups. The betsimisaraka people live on the east coast. The word translates as 'the inseparable many.' They have often made a living from the sea, as fishermen, whalers, sailors and pirates.

✸ **Bokiboky**: The narrow-striped mongoose found in Madagascar.

✸ **Booty**: treasure, stolen goods.

✸ **Bowsprit**: a spar or pole that juts out from the front of a ship.

☠ **Breeches**: trousers that reach to the knee.

☠ **Brigantine**: a two-masted sailing ship.

☠ **Buccaneer**: a pirate, originally one operating in the Caribbean.

☠ **Cravat**: a wide piece of fabric worn at the neck, a bit like a tie.

☠ **Cutlass**: a short sword with a slightly curved blade.

☠ **Dokotera**: Malagasy word for Doctor.

☠ **Elephant Bird**: A type of large, flightless bird (extinct) from Madagascar.

☠ **Fanaloka**: a nocturnal striped civet found in Madagascar.

☠ **Flintlock**: an old-fashioned type of gun fired by a spark from a flint.

☠ **Fossa**: Madagascar's largest carnivorous mammal.

☠ **Furled**: neatly rolled up.

☠ **Gaff sail**: a large sail with four corners.

☠ **Galley**: the ship's kitchen.

☠ **Gangway**: a raised platform or walkway providing passage to a ship.

☠ **Gecko**: a colourful small lizard found in Madagascar.

☠ **Gibbet**: A cage like contraption used to publicly display the remains of someone who was executed.

☠ **Hardtack**: hard dry biscuit or cracker, given as rations to sailors.

☠ **Hatches**: an opening in the deck of a ship.

☠ **Jib sail**: a triangular sail.

☠ **Keelhaul**: a gruesome punishment where a person is dragging through the water under the bottom of a ship.

☠ **Knapsack**: A bag carried on a person's back.

☠ **Lamba shawl**: a large wrap resembling a shawl that is worn by Malagasy people and is made of various fabrics in solid colours or patterns.

☠ **Lasopy**: traditional Malagasy soup.

☠ **Mainmast**: the principal mast of a ship, typically the second mast in a sailing ship of three or more masts.

☠ **Maki**: Malagasy name for ring-tailed lemur

☠ **Malagasy**: a person born in Madagascar.

🕱 **Mbola tsara**: Greeting similar to 'hello' (coastal dialect.)

🕱 **Menagerie**: a collection of wild animals kept in captivity for exhibition.

🕱 **Merchant ship**: a ship used to transport cargo.

🕱 **Misaotra**: Malagasy word meaning thank you.

🕱 **Mutiny**: an open rebellion by sailors against their captain.

🕱 **Nosy Boraha**: small island off the east cost of Madagascar also known as Ile Sainte Marie.

🕱 **Pirogue**: a long, narrow canoe made from a tree trunk.

🕱 **Ratlines**: (pronounced ratlins) ropes used for climbing the rigging.

🕱 **Rigging**: ropes, chains and tackle used to control the masts, yardarms and sails on a ship.

🕱 **Sextant**: A navigational instrument used to navigate by the stars.

🕱 **Ship's head**: A box like structure next to the bowsprit used as a toilet. The box has slots in the bottom to allow the sea water below to act as a flush.

🕱 **Shrouds**: vertical rigging that hold up the mast.

Slops: sailor's clothing.

Stalactites: an icicle-like calcium salt formation deposited by dripping water. They are found hanging down from cave roofs.

Stalagmites: an icicle-like calcium salt formation deposited by dripping water. They are found rising up from the floor of caves.

Stern: the back of the ship.

Spyglass: a small telescope.

Tapers: a slender candle.

Tenrec: a small insectivorous mammal found in Madagascar, different kinds of which resemble hedgehogs or mice.

Three-cornered-hat: a hat with the brim turned up and pinned on three sides often worn by pirates.

Tureen: a serving dish for foods such as soups or stews.

Votsotsa: Malagasy giant jumping rat.

Vontsira: A ring-tailed mongoose found in Madagascar.

Weevil: any small insect that damages stored grain.

Yam: A root vegetable/edible tuber.

Zebu: Omby in Malagasy – a domestic cattle with a large hump.

AUTHOR'S NOTE

This book is inspired by the 'Golden Age of Piracy' between the 1650s and the 1730s. Many people associate pirates with the Caribbean – perhaps because of a famous film series! But I was especially fascinated to learn there was a Pirate Island, just four miles of the East coast off Madagascar. Nosy Boraha (Ile Sainte Marie) and the tiny Pirate Island which sits in its harbour seemed the perfect setting for a pirate book!

There is thought to have been up to 1,500 pirates living on Nosy Boraha, but by the late 1700s there was only around 100. Some may have been buried on the island. The Pirate Cemetery exists, and some headstones do feature skulls and/or crossbones.

There are three captain's in *Kintana and the Captain's Curse* – and two of them are based on actual pirates.

Captain Blackbeard – real name Edward Teach – was born in Bristol, England in around 1680. He served in the Royal Navy, but later became a pirate, mainly causing havoc in the Caribbean. He really did tie fuses in his hair and beard, lighting them so the smoke would billow and terrify his enemies.

In 1718 Blackbeard faced a deadly sword dual at the Battle of Okracoke, North Carolina, USA. In his fatal, final fight he received 25 wounds, including five gunshots.

After his death, Blackbeard's decapitated head was tied to the ship's bowsprit as a warning to other pirates in the area. Later, stories abounded that Blackbeard's headless body swam around the coast looking for his head!

Captain William Kidd was born in Dundee, Scotland, in 1655.

Kidd was employed as a pirate hunter, but apparently wasn't very good at his job! His crew grew mutinous and forced Kidd to turn pirate. They took the *Quedah Merchant*, a ship with a rich cargo of cloth, opium, iron and saltpeter (a vital component in gunpowder.) Kidd renamed the ship *The Adventure*, but unfortunately, she was rotten and leaky. He stripped the ship of anything of value, and then scuttled her – deliberately sinking her off the north east coast of Madagascar near Nosy Boraha.

Kidd was pardoned for being a pirate, and sailed on to Boston, USA, but there he was arrested and sent back to England to face trial. The evidence was heard quickly, and Kidd was found guilty. He was sentenced to hang, but his execution did not go smoothly. On the first attempt the rope around Kidd's neck broke. He was strung up a second time, but this time it worked. His corpse was placed in a gibbet at the mouth of the River Thames, London, as a warning to other pirates.

There is a third character based on a real person – Israel Hands. Israel worked alongside Blackbeard, possibly as his First Mate. He was shot in the knee by his captain during a card game – with Teach reportedly saying "If I do not now and then kill one of them, they would forget who I was."

The injury meant that Israel was recovering elsewhere when Blackbeard was attacked and killed at Okracoke. Afterwards anyone linked to Blackbeard was put on trial for piracy. Because Israel was not at the battle, it was hard to prove him guilty. He turned King's Witness and gave evidence against the men who had been receiving Blackbeard's stolen goods. He is believed to have spent four months in prison – but his life after that remains a mystery. The only clue, a story that he ended up in London, begging for bread. I imagined he might have started a new life on Pirate Island.

I am not the only author to have been inspired by Israel Hands – he also features in Robert Louis Stevenson's *Treasure Island*.

I have really enjoyed researching pirates and was thrilled to discover despite superstitions about females on board ship, that there were women pirates – most famously Anne Bonny and Mary Read. I was surprised however to learn that there is no evidence that anyone was ever forced to walk the plank – but I couldn't resist using my own version of the punishment!

Madagascar is the fourth largest island in the world. It split from the African continent an estimated 160 million years ago.

The island is home to 25,000 species of animal and most are endemic – meaning they aren't found anywhere else.

All the animals and plants in *Kintana and the Captain's Curse* are real, although not all are found on Nosy Boraha. I did allow myself a little artistic licence – for example having a pygmy hippo in the pet shop and resurrecting giant sloth lemurs and elephant birds – all three once roamed Madagascar but have been extinct for thousands of years! Vasa parrots, unlike African greys, cannot speak – but females really do lose their feathers revealing their yellow head!

The aye-aye is an endangered species. It has been struggling because of habitat loss. Some Malagasy also believe that sight of this nocturnal lemur can foretell sickness and death. Sometimes they are killed as a way of lifting the omen. However, superstitions are changing and there are increasing efforts by Malagasy and conservation groups to protect this unique lemur.

ACKNOWLEDGEMENTS

Kintana and the Captain's Curse has a long history. It was my first attempt at a children's book and was originally inspired when I discovered my sister was pregnant. I decided to write a book for the baby. Max is now 20! So, thank you Karen and Max for your patience and for setting me off on the path of becoming a children's author.

A big hello to everyone at Blackpool Zoo, especially the education team members I worked with in 2012. It was a real privilege to spend a season with you teaching visitors about the fabulous animals – and so much fun! My encounters with the ring-tailed lemurs, giant hissing cockroaches and Darwin the giant tortoise played an important part in the writing of this book.

I would also like to thank Dr Lee Durrell for responding to my research query about Madagascar animals.

I am especially grateful to Dr Phil Boyle, former Ambassador to Madagascar, for his very generous feedback on my manuscript. Thank you, Phil, for your insightful comments on Malagasy culture and your shared expertise on Madagascar wildlife.

Huge thanks also to Shaun Reveley and Nicole Ralay for reading my manuscript and offering feedback on Malagasy culture, language and the geography of Nosy Boraha.

Thank you also to Daniel Austin, secretary of the Anglo Malagasy Society and Vaonarivo Brown for assistance with finding a Malagasy sensitivity reader and for advice on Betsimisaraka culture.

I would like to thank Ishbel Kargar and the OWLS (now

Ormskirk Writers) writing group, Ruth Symes and Heidi Schultz and Louise Jordan of the Writers' Advice Centre for their encouragement and feedback on very early drafts.

As always, a huge shout out to my SCBWI friends especially Anna Mainwaring, Catherine Whitmore, Faye Sunderland, Georgina Blair, Mel Green, Barbara Henderson, Ruth Estevez, Dom Conlon, Marie Basting, Lois Johnson, Jayne Fallows and Cath Nichols. Big thanks to Louise Jones for beta reading both Gracie Fairshaw and Kintana! Your comments were so helpful!

Huge thanks to Jade Derricott, Gabrielle-Star Swales and Ellie Sime for helping transform my manuscript. You have been incredible, especially given the challenges of trying to complete an MA in lockdown! I am sure you have wonderful careers ahead of you.

Thank you to Kathy Webb for her fabulous edits and support, and patiently schooling me on grammar!

Thank you to the wonderful, super-talented Jenny Czerwonka for creating another super cover and wonderful animal illustrations, under direction from the UcLan students.

Thanks also to Becky Chilcott for her assistance with the cover design.

Thank you to everyone at UcLan Publishing including Alexa Gregson-Kenmuir, Charlotte Rothwell, Toni Murtagh and especially Hazel Holmes. You are the best!

I am extremely grateful to all the booksellers, bloggers, magazine editors, librarians, journalists, fellow authors, SCBWI and Get Blackpool Reading who have supported my books, for opportunities and helping with marketing, promotion and sales. Thanks especially to Tony Higginson (Beyond Books

Media) for organising my first virtual school visits and Bounce Marketing.

Finally, a big thank you to my family, friends and colleagues for your support, it means so much to me.

ABOUT THE AUTHOR

SUSAN BROWNRIGG is passionate about history and wildlife. She has worked for a number of heritage visitor attractions as a living history presenter and now works full time as a museum learning manager. She worked for a summer season at Blackpool Zoo and particularly enjoyed delivering talks about the giant tortoise and lemurs (even when the ring-tail lemurs sat on her head!)

Susan is a former journalist and sub-editor. She was awarded the Margaret Carey Scholarship in 2015 and was chosen as a SCBWI Undiscovered Voices winner in 2016. Her debut children's book *Gracie Fairshaw and the Mysterious Guest* is also published by UcLan Publishing.

IF YOU LIKED THIS,
YOU'LL LOVE . . .

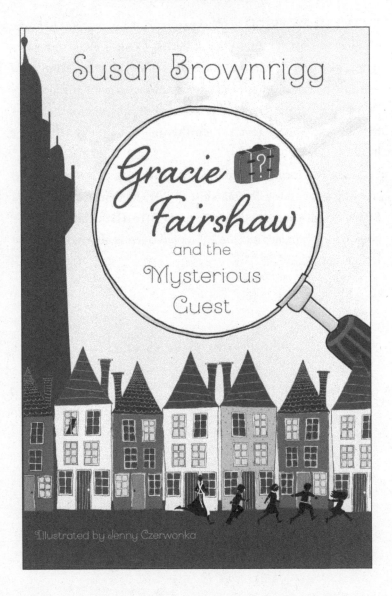

Susan Brownrigg

Gracie
Fairshaw
and the
Mysterious
Guest

Illustrated by Jenny Czerwonka